THE STEM NiGHT DiSASTeR

DR. KATE BIBERDORF
WITH HILLARY HOMZIE

Philomel Books

Hi! My Name is Dr. Kate Biberdorf,

but most people call me Kate the Chemist. I perform explosive science experiments on national TV when I'm not in Austin, Texas, teaching chemistry classes. Besides being the best science in the entire world, chemistry is the study of energy and matter, and their interactions with each other. Like how I can use limes to power a calculator or liquid nitrogen to make a thundercloud! If you read *The STEM Night Disaster* carefully, you will see how Little Kate the Chemist uses chemistry to solve problems in her everyday life.

But remember, none of the experiments in this book should be done without the supervision of a trained professional! If you are looking for some fun, safe, at-home experiments, check out my companion book, *Kate the Chemist: The Big Book of Experiments*. (I've included one experiment from that book in the back of this one—how to make a lemon battery!)

And one more thing: Science is all about making predictions (or forming hypotheses), which you can do right now! Will Little Kate the Chemist and Birdie be able to use their science skills to save STEM Night? Let's find out—it's time for Kate the Chemist's third adventure.

XOXO,
Kate

ALSO BY DR. KATE BIBERDORF

Kate the Chemist: The Big Book of Experiments

Kate the Chemist: Dragons vs. Unicorns

Kate the Chemist: The Great Escape

PHILOMEL BOOKS
An imprint of Penguin Random House LLC, New York

First published in the United States of America by Philomel,
an imprint of Penguin Random House LLC, 2021.

Visit us online at penguinrandomhouse.com.

Library of Congress Cataloging-in-Publication Data is available.

Printed in the United States of America

ISBN 9780593116616

1 3 5 7 9 10 8 6 4 2

Edited by Jill Santopolo.

Designed by Lori Thorn.

Text set in ITC Stone Serif.

For Cheryl, Hillary, and Jill,

the three amazing women who helped me bring the

Kate the Chemist series to life

TABLE OF CONTENTS

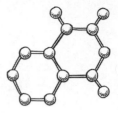

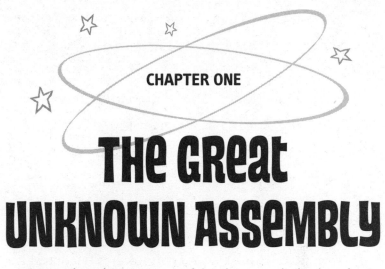

CHAPTER ONE

THE GREAT UNKNOWN ASSEMBLY

Inference (noun). The process of drawing a conclusion based on evidence. Like if your little brother has cheeks full of crumbs, you can infer that he just ate the last cookie.

WAITING WAS TORTURE. The entire fifth grade sat in the auditorium. Any moment the administration was supposed to make a huge announcement. I bounced in my seat. I twirled my hair. I sucked in my cheeks.

"C'mon, Kate," said Elijah Williams, one of my closest friends. "Tell us what's going on."

"I wish I knew." I had to practically shout. All around us students were chatting and chairs were squeaking so loudly I could barely hear.

Birdie Bhatt studied the white cinder-block walls. "Maybe we're going to paint a giant mural." This didn't surprise me. Birdie and I had been BFFs since kindergarten, and she was all about art.

Next to me, Memito Alvarez patted his middle. "I hope they're going to announce a cooking club."

"Doubtful." Avery Cooper shook her head and her blonde braids swayed. "I think they're going to make the cafeteria go completely green. My student council committee has already drawn up a proposal."

"No plastic straws or paper napkins," explained Phoenix Altman from the row in front of us. "And more options for vegetarians."

"I'm fine as long as there are no Brussels sprouts." Jeremy Rowe leaned back in his chair. "Bet you a dollar none of you are right," he said, smirking.

"I haven't guessed anything yet." Elijah pointed in my direction. "I'm going to go with whatever Kate thinks. 'Cause of Mrs. Crawford."

Of course, at that moment, it got quiet enough so

everyone could hear Elijah. All the kids looked at me. Even the rows farther away.

That was because *Mrs. Crawford* happened to be the principal of Rosalind Franklin Elementary School. And she also happened to be my mother. But truly, I had no idea what was going on.

Ms. Gottfried, the librarian, who was our audio-visual guru, adjusted the height of a microphone in front of the stage area. A banner below the scoreboard read: *Today is THE day!*

"C'mon, Kate," insisted Elijah. "Tell us what's up."

I wracked my brain. "I really don't know."

"What does your gut tell you?" Phoenix leaned forward, her parrot earrings swishing.

"That I'm super hungry," joked Memito. "I only had one waffle for breakfast and it's almost lunchtime."

We all laughed.

"Just guess what you think is going to happen, Kate," pleaded Elijah.

"Scientists don't guess," I said in my most patient voice. Elijah, who is my next-door neighbor, has heard me say this about a billion times before. "Guesses are often random."

You see, I'm interested in science—chemistry, especially. Actually, strike that. I'm obsessed. Because chemistry is everything. It's everywhere. It's how your stomach breaks down the candy bar you've just inhaled. How laundry detergent scrubs the dirt off your socks. Why popcorn pops in your microwave and tastes so yummy.

Birdie gently poked me. "Then make a hypothesis."

A hypothesis is an explanation that can be tested. I think about the most recent observations I've made surrounding the mystery at our school. Unfortunately, I haven't had time to test out anything.

"I could make an inference." I shrugged. "You know, come up with an idea based on evidence."

Ms. Gottfried tapped the microphone. "Testing," she said. "Testing, one. Two. Three." The microphone wasn't working. We could barely hear Ms. Gottfried's voice from across the auditorium.

Kids whipped around to look up front. Some students in the back were getting squirmy. The chatter in the room grew louder.

Jeremy's gaze followed the teachers scurrying up

4

front with clipboards. "The assembly is going to start any second," he said. "If you want to win the bet, you've got to make your predictions right now."

"You mean, make an inference." I grinned at him.

"Yeah, yeah, whatever." Jeremy shrugged. "An inference, then."

That got me thinking about all of the observations I had made in the past week. I definitely knew there was a mystery going on around school. And I was about to use my powers of observation to figure it out!

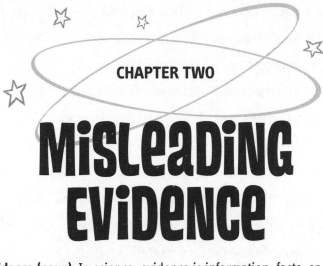

MiSLEADING EViDENCE

Evidence (noun). In science, evidence is information, facts, or data that support a hypothesis or claim. Like when your little brother has cheeks full of chocolate crumbs, and the last brownie went missing—the evidence would be the chocolate crumbs.

THE CLUES TO THE MYSTERY at Rosalind Franklin Elementary were everywhere. I considered the evidence. First of all, there were new signs put up last week. As in actual signs.

1) In the library, a giant banner read: **Be curious.**

I ask so many questions, curious could be my middle name. Kate Curious Crawford. (My real middle name is Alexis, which I think sounds like a type of car.)

2) Next to the water fountain by the front office, a poster read: **Are you ready?**

I like to think I was born ready. At least, that's what my soccer coach always says. But the truth is I'm more like just on time or even one to two minutes late, because I'm always trying to do one more thing before I have to leave.

3) By the lost and found closet, a banner read: **Be positive.**

Maybe this meant, *Don't worry. You probably didn't lose your water bottle. Check the lost and found closet!* I seriously hate to misplace anything. Once I lost a mitten and I searched for half a day by the pond. Luckily, I found it under a pine tree.

4) By the teacher's lounge, a sign read: **Have a growth mindset.**

That doesn't mean you're supposed to suddenly sprout up like a mushroom. Mom loved to talk about this saying after she went to a conference last summer. She told me it meant you should be up for challenges and believe in hard work. My soccer coach says that *good things come to those who sweat!* I think it's kind of the same thing.

I reviewed all of the signs. *Be curious. Are you ready? Be positive* and *Have a growth mindset.*

Aha! A pattern had emerged. I could see what all the messages had in common.

"I've come up with something," I announced to my friends.

"Awesome!" Elijah drummed his hands on his chair.

"The anticipation is killing me," moaned Memito.

"Based on the evidence." I spread out my hands. "I think they're going to announce a mindfulness assembly. So we can learn breathing exercises that teachers hope will calm us down in class."

Memito pretended to snore. In the chair in front of him, Rory Workman cradled his head and also went, "Zzzzzzzz."

"Hey, I like meditating. I do it with my uncle," said Elijah.

"Sitting around and learning how to breathe, really?" Jeremy snort-laughed. "Kate, you're going to lose the bet. All of you are going down."

"Sorry, there's a hitch in your bet plan." I stared at Jeremy as he flicked his bangs with the dyed purple streak in them. "You never said what you think."

"I don't have to guess," he huffed. "I'm betting you guys are wrong."

My mother stepped up to the microphone and tapped it. The mic made a loud pop. "Good morning, fifth graders," she said.

Jeremy and Rory continued talking.

"Zip it," I blurted.

Oops! I hope the principal, aka my mom, didn't hear me say *zip it*.

I try not to blurt stuff out.

But sometimes I can't help it.

Mom held up her hand as if she were stopping traffic. "It's time for our assembly."

Immediately the room grew silent. "Look how quickly you were quiet," she continued. "That's amazing."

Kids cheered.

"We have a super fun assembly planned for you today," said Mom. "We're going to be kicking off something new."

"What is it?" called out Rory.

"You'll see," said Mom. "And here's the person to tell you all about it." She stepped away from the microphone.

Ms. Daly, the chemistry club advisor, burst out from behind the stage curtain. She wore a baseball cap over her short gray hair. The hat said CHEMISTS HAVE ALL THE SOLUTIONS. Which was typical of her awesome corny humor.

In her arms, she carried a big blue bucket the size of a kindergartner. It wasn't a bucket I recognized. Since I never miss a chemistry club meeting, I pretty much know all of the equipment in our school lab.

"What do you think is in there?" whispered Birdie. "Some kind of chemical?"

"Maybe," I whispered back.

With a heave, Ms. Daly dumped the bucket upside down.

Ping-pong balls exploded out, hitting the floor with a series of clacking sounds. They rolled right up to our rows of chairs.

Rory reached so far to grab one that he fell off and his seat flipped up. Kids laughed and I had to hold back a gasp. Not because he fell. But because if anyone was going to have their seat flip up, it would have been

Jeremy. Birdie and I scrambled to pick a couple of balls careening down the center aisle.

I scooped up a bright yellow one. In small writing, it read: *STEM Night begins Nov. 20!*

"STEM Night?" I whisper-shouted to Birdie. "Yes! Yes!"

"Kate guessed wrong," sang out Jeremy. "And Memito, you were wrong too. And Birdie."

"Quiet back there," called out Ms. Daly.

"I'm never wrong," said Memito.

Essh! I don't like being wrong. But if science is involved, I'm kind of okay with it.

Ms. Daly began chanting, "One, two, three, eyes on me."

"One, two, eyes on you," we chanted back. It's a thing we do at our school when a teacher needs to get our attention.

"For the first time ever, Rosalind Franklin Elementary School is going to have a community-wide STEM Night," explained Ms. Daly. "There's going to be hands-on science activities for families to do together, and a science project exhibit area open to fifth graders only."

"Fifth graders? That's us!" A huge smile spread across Elijah's face. A ginormous one was on mine, too.

"The event will happen in three weeks," continued Ms. Daly. "The science projects are mandatory and must include original experiments."

Suddenly, Mrs. Eberlin, my fifth-grade teacher, and Mrs. Que, the other fifth grade teacher, waltzed up onstage. They both wore blue lab coats and goggles and were dancing to loud, happy music playing over the speakers.

"Yup, you guys are going to rock your science projects," said Ms. Daly as our teachers continued to boogie. Kids laughed and clapped their hands in time to the music as Mrs. Eberlin twirled around Mrs. Que.

Ms. Daly raised her hands over her head. "Let's hear it for science!"

We cheered. I yelled my head off. This was like a pep rally for science.

Projected on the wall above the stage, giant words appeared. They said: GUESS WHO'S COMING.

"On STEM Night, someone special will visit Franklin

Elementary," said Ms. Daly. "And I've got to emphasize the word *special*."

Who could it be?

A scientist? An engineer? An inventor?

"The next slide will reveal the answer," Ms. Daly said. We all leaned forward, waiting.

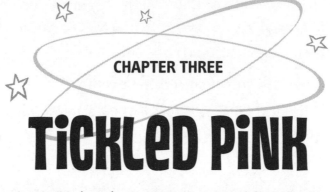

CHAPTER THREE

TiCKLeD PiNK

Potassium iodide (noun). A white salt made up of crystals. It's used in photography and the medical field. It turns yellow because it reacts with the oxygen and carbon dioxide in the air. I guess then you could call it mellow yellow.

THE SLIDE SHOWED A SCIENTIST in a hot pink lab coat, her arms raised in a champion salute. Her eyes shone behind pink goggles.

For a moment, there was a stunned silence.

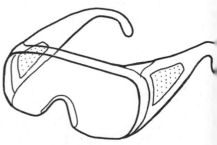

I definitely recognized that lab coat. And those goggles.

"Dr. Caroline!" I shrieked, popping out of my seat.

Kids whispered and pointed at Dr. Caroline's picture. Others stood up and cheered.

And I was cheering the loudest.

Dr. Caroline is my favorite scientist on YouTube. She does all of these really cool demos. My favorite is how she makes puking pumpkins using a solution of hydrogen peroxide and dish soap, just like we did with Ms. Daly at the Fall Festival this year. I learn something new every time I watch Dr. Caroline. With the puking pumpkins, I learned about catalysts, things that speed up a chemical reaction. In this case, the catalyst was potassium iodide. So cool!

I've watched all of the episodes on her channel at least a dozen times.

Okay, sometimes more. I've pretty much memorized them.

I'm pretty much her number one fan.

Suddenly, my mom headed back to the microphone with a really wide smile. "I have some wonderful news," she trilled.

Hard to believe there could be anything more after this.

"Our school has won a special community grant, which is allowing us to fly Dr. Caroline here to judge the science projects and get you guys all fired up about science," said Mom.

I turned to Birdie and she turned to me. We both mouthed "no way" at the same time.

"And the best part," continued Mom. "The winner of the competition will get a thousand dollars to do something special for the school. Second place will get five hundred dollars, and third place will get two hundred and fifty dollars. So our whole school community will benefit from this grant, not just because we get to meet Dr. Caroline and have our very first STEM Night, but because three of you will get to choose a special way to make our school better for years to come!"

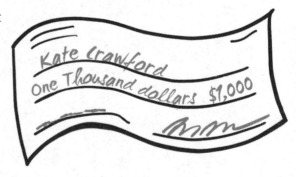

Kate Crawford
One Thousand dollars $1,000

I jumped up and down like I was on a trampoline. The clapping in the auditorium grew louder.

STEM Night. A science competition AND I was

going to meet Dr. Caroline live-and-in-person.

Sure, I might have lost Jeremy's dumb bet. But that was okay.

Because from my point of view, I had already won something much better than any bet.

CHAPTER FOUR

BOUNCING IDEAS

Science demonstration (noun). Introducing or explaining a principle of science through a visual example so others can see it firsthand. Like you might create an eruption in a papier-mâché volcano with vinegar and baking soda to demonstrate an acid-base chemical reaction.

I FLIPPED THROUGH A CHEMISTRY BOOK, searching for the perfect experiment or demo. "Are you guys having any luck finding a project?"

"Not yet." Birdie thumbed through *The Big Book of Totally Awesome Science Experiments*, which was propped on her lap. Right after the assembly, Birdie and I had grabbed a bunch of science books from the school library to look for the perfect experiments together. Elijah and

Memito had been hanging out at Elijah's house after school but had come over when they saw me and Birdie on my back patio. Elijah's yard is right next to mine so it's easy for him to hop over the chain-link fence. Now we were all sprawled on lawn chairs in my backyard.

"I don't need luck," said Memito. "I've got my project all figured out. I'm going to test different ways to dry mango and figure out which method tastes the best." He licked his lips.

"I'm coming over to your house, so I can be a taste tester," said Elijah.

"And celebrate me coming in first." Memito rubbed his hands together. "I'm going to use the prize money to start a cooking club."

Elijah tapped on a tree stump. "Bet you can't guess what I'm going to do. Oops, sorry—I mean make an inference." He grinned.

"Something with drumming obviously," I said.

"Give that girl a pair of drumsticks," said Elijah. "I'm going to use different sticks on my drums and figure out which one creates the best sound quality. And since I'm going to win, I'll use the money to start a battle of the bands." Elijah elbowed me. "What's your experiment,

Kate? I bet you already have yours all typed and printed out already."

"Actually," I said, "I haven't figured it out yet. The problem is, there are just so many things I'm curious about." I peered up at the sky. "Like why is it blue up there? I'm not sure, but I have ideas. I know it has something to do with chemistry—all the particles and gases in the air." I pointed to a maple leaf that was bright red. "Why is that red? I know it's chemistry."

"So basically, you come up with an experiment about anything that makes you curious," said Birdie.

"Exactly!" I said. "It just has to be awesome for Dr. Caroline. I still have no clue what I would do with a thousand dollars though."

I glanced over at Birdie, who had a mysterious smile on her face. "You figured out something," I said.

"Yup." Birdie peered up from one of our science experiment books. "I want to use the prize money to paint a mural on the library wall."

"And what about your project?" I asked.

"Not sure." She started flipping through her book again. Then she came to a picture that made her gasp. "That's so pretty." It was a spread featuring colorful strips of paper towels hanging on a clothesline. "They look tie dyed. It's called an ink chromatography experiment. You get to separate colors." Her fingertips slowly brushed the image as if ink might somehow come off the page. "I think I've found my experiment!"

"Still don't know what you want to do, Kate?" asked Elijah in a teasing voice.

"No," I admitted. "Not yet." I pointed to our trampoline. "Let's stop talking. And go jumping."

Everyone rushed over.

Birdie grabbed my hand and we jumped together while Elijah and Memito started tossing as many balls as they could find onto the trampoline. It was like jumping in a hot air popcorn popper, only without the hot air. And without the kernels.

After a big flip, I thought about how electrons move around an atom, sometimes in unpredictable ways just like the balls. Maybe I could make a miniature trampoline to demonstrate how electrons bopped around.

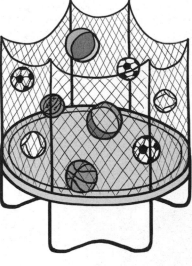

I peered up at that blue atmosphere. "Maybe I could do a chromatography test of the sky," I said with a wink.

"Ha ha," said Birdie.

"I don't know," I said with a giant jump, "with chemistry anything is possible."

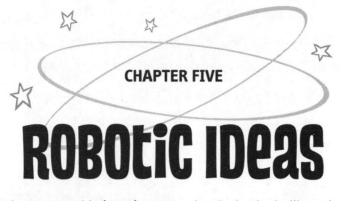

CHAPTER FIVE

ROBOtiC IDEAS

Hydrogen peroxide (noun). It's a molecule that looks like a clear, bubbly liquid and has the molecular formula H_2O_2. It kills lots of germs and that's why it's found in some mouthwash. But it's more famous for whitening teeth than getting rid of stinky smells.

IN THE FAMILY ROOM, I watched a Dr. Caroline video. Mom had a school board meeting and Dad was working in his office. My little brother Liam was fiddling with his remote-control robot on the floor next to me.

"Do you think I could get my robot to jump up a ladder and get stuff?" asked Liam. "Like cookies?"

I glanced up from the iPad on my lap. "Not unless you can program him."

"His name is Norbert."

"Sorry—Norbert. Plus, he'd have to be engineered with different legs in order to climb."

"Aw, man. Why couldn't they have done that?" With a sigh, Liam waggled the robot's legs.

"Sometimes you can't always figure stuff out." But that couldn't be the case with my science project. Today was Sunday and it had been almost a week since the assembly announcing STEM Night. And I still didn't know what to do. That's why I was binge watching.

Dr. Caroline was making something called Elephant's Toothpaste. I guess because it was big and bubbly enough to clean an elephant's mouth. It was the first of her videos I had ever seen and it's still one of my favorites. She takes 35% hydrogen peroxide (H_2O_2), potassium iodide, dish soap, and food coloring to make the most awesome, explosive, mushy reaction ever.

On-screen, Dr. Caroline stared

24

at the orange fluffy stuff coming out of the Erlenmeyer flask. "Isn't that cool?" she yelled.

"Yes!" I yelled back.

Behind her, a poster read: I'M POSITIVE I'VE LOST MY ELECTRON.

I was positive that I loved Dr. Caroline.

Suddenly I felt a pinch on my arm. "Ow!" I whipped around to see Norbert's robot hand on my elbow.

Liam was beaming. "You said you wanted to pinch yourself. So I got Norbert to do it."

"What do you mean?"

"I heard you talking with Birdie the other day. You said you wanted to pinch yourself 'cause you're going to meet Dr. Caroline."

I started giggling. Sometimes I forget that Liam is just a kindergartner. After explaining what I meant, we both cracked up. Then he got interested in Norbert knocking down blocks.

I went back to watching more videos. In one of them, Dr. Caroline made a pink solution turn completely clear by blowing carbon dioxide into it with a giant straw. In another one, Dr. Caroline used limes to power a digital clock. In still another one, she made a Rube Goldberg machine, which is a series of chain reactions that do a simple thing in a ridiculously complex way. It all started with a phone buzzing that knocked into a row of dominoes, setting off a chain reaction involving pulleys, levers, bells, and ending in a test tube filled with vinegar being dumped into a papier-mâché volcano that exploded.

Something just had to spark an idea. My project needed to be fun and exciting, but with really interesting science if it was going to win. And I wanted it to feel like mine. Something original that came from me.

By my feet, a bunch of blocks knocked to the floor with a soft thud. Norbert and Liam were definitely up to their usual tricks.

Looking down, I noticed tiny screws in Norbert's battery compartment gleaming under the light. Wait a minute! His toy used a battery that was easy to take out. This gave me an idea. A lime battery, but better! "For my project, I could power your robot with fruit, Liam. Maybe I could figure out how to make him do something cool like write a word. Or do something else awesome."

"Yeah, just do something cool and show me how to do it, too."

I slapped his hand. "A high five," I said, "for a five-year-old."

He put his chubby arms around me for a hug.

I hugged him back. This could totally work. It would impress Ms. Daly *and* Dr. Caroline. It would be the best science project at STEM Night.

Now I just had to figure out what to do with the prize money. Because I knew I was going to win!

CHAPTER SIX

POWER UP!

Biodegradation (noun). A chemical process where matter is broken down by microorganisms like fungi. Fungi is the plural of fungus. This gives a whole new meaning to "there's a fungus among us."

ON MONDAY AFTERNOON, Ms. Daly stood in the front of the science lab. It was after lunch, and everyone in my class was working on their STEM projects. "I'm going to give you"—she glanced at her watch—"a few more minutes to get organized. And then I want everyone to show off your materials and how you plan to use them with group members."

Oh, I couldn't wait to do that! The class had been

split into five groups. Ms. Daly put me with Jeremy, Memito, and Phoenix. The idea was that we were supposed to think through our projects together. And help each other, if we needed it.

At the next table, Birdie was with Elijah, Avery, and Rory. I waved at her. And she waved back. I wished I could be with her.

"When one of you is demonstrating your project," said Ms. Daly, holding up a pencil, "the rest of you will write down observations. For example, you could write, 'I see a clear liquid.' When everyone is finished, hand in your notes. That means even when it's not your turn to present, you'll be actively learning and participating."

"Will we be tested on this?" asked Avery in a worried voice. She's pretty competitive when it comes to grades.

I guess I am, too.

"Nope, no quiz," said Ms. Daly. "But I will give everyone participation points."

Lots of kids sighed with relief.

While we set up our materials, everyone in my group started talking about what they'd do with the money if they won on STEM night. Which wasn't actually that far away, just eleven days.

"I'd use the prize money to get new soccer goals for the school," said Jeremy.

"Soccer is great," said Phoenix. "But we already have cones. They work fine. I think we need to buy some big composting bins for the garden."

"Actually, we need to get more raised garden beds, to supply veggies for the cooking club," said Memito. "Which we'll definitely need to start."

"Kate, what are you going to do with your money, if you win?" asked Jeremy.

"I don't know." I flipped through my binder. "I'm still trying to figure it out."

Out of the corner of my eye, I watched Ms. Gottfried, our librarian, stroll into the lab. A black camera with a maroon strap hung around her neck. "Don't mind me, everyone," she said. "I'm taking photos and video for our school website."

Soon enough, I was scribbling furious notes while I listened to Phoenix. She held up a 2-liter soda bottle that had been cut in half so the bottom could serve as a stand for the top half turned upside down. Dirt, orange peels, and shredded napkins filled the inside.

Memito held his nose. "That's stinky."

30

"It's kind of awesome," said Jeremy.

"I agree!" I wrote: awesome way to recycle a bottle.

"I want to dump that bottle on my brother's pillow," said Jeremy with a sly smile.

"It's not something to just throw away," sniffed Phoenix. "Everything comes from the earth. And most of it can be recycled, reused, or composted. If you throw it into a landfill, it just sits there."

As Phoenix stirred the dirt with a spoon, I studied the criteria judges would be using to evaluate our projects. They would be looking at 1) scientific thought, 2) thoroughness, 3) demonstrated skills, and 4) our ability to communicate our project and make STEM connections. There was no doubt that Phoenix would be able to do all of that. I couldn't get jealous. Scientists need to support each other.

I pointed at the compost pail. "Hey, that's cool chemistry!" I motioned over to Ms. Gottfried. "You should get a photo of this."

Ms. Gottfried glided closer. Pushing up her aqua-colored glasses on her nose, she grinned. "Good idea." Then I could hear her camera going *click, click, click.*

"Kate's right," said Phoenix. "Composting is

chemistry. According to my research, biodegradation is a chemical process where stuff is broken down by microorganisms like bacteria. But only some things break down that way." She pointed to pieces of plastic in the pail. "That's why I cut up lids from yogurt cartons. I predict they won't get broken down."

Memito winced and wrote down in giant letters: **can be stinky.**

"Sure you're not talking about your socks?" teased Phoenix.

"My socks and your dirt," said Memito. During his turn, he held up a bag of dried fruit, and my stomach tightened. His project looked so far along.

"Did you already finish your project?" asked Jeremy, who had been reading my thoughts.

"Yup," said Memito. "I was so excited to get started."

While he talked about the science of drying fruit, I tried to contain my worry about being behind. Instead, I focused on the fact that Ms. Gottfried was now filming Birdie. Yay Birdie! She was talking about her chromatography project.

I wanted to clap when Birdie held up her project, which almost looked like a tie-dye cloth, with splashes of sea blue, plum, and hot pink. She had just as many colors as Avery, who sat next to her with jars of DIY lip gloss.

"Ahem," grumbled Memito, poking me in the shoulder.

"Oh, sorry!" I whirled back around.

Memito waved a baggie of dried mangos. "Don't you want some?"

"Sure!" I grabbed a morsel of fruit leather. "Mmm, this tastes so perfect."

"Thanks," said Memito. "Which means I'm not going to put it anywhere near that bottle of dirt."

"Compost," corrected Phoenix.

"Okay, everyone, it's fruit-powered battery time." I waved my arms. "Hey, Ms. Gottfried. Do you want to see the true power of a lemon?" I pointed to the one on the table. "Get ready!"

CHAPTER SEVEN

A FRUITFUL SEARCH

Power (noun). How fast energy is transferred from one spot to another. The faster something gets transferred, the more power. So, think of it as a faster runner in a race having more power than a slowpoke.

"THIS IS GOING TO BE SO COOL," I said, fiddling with the arms of Liam's robot. "I'm using a piece of fruit to power up my little brother's favorite toy." I moved the little levers.

Everyone in my STEM group leaned forward for a better look.

"Whoa! That's amazing," exclaimed Memito.

"Thanks." I hadn't tried out the battery yet and was eager to get started. I couldn't believe how far ahead both Phoenix and Memito were. And Birdie and Avery, too, from the looks of it. I didn't like feeling behind.

As Avery walked by to sharpen her pencil, she studied the lemon and then the robot. "Is that really going to work?" she asked.

"Oh yeah!" I promised.

Ms. Gottfried strode closer to get a close-up on the lemon. Turning, I gave her my best smile.

"My dad calls his car a lemon," said Jeremy. "But turning an actual lemon into a battery? That doesn't seem possible."

"Come closer." I motioned to Ms. Gottfried. "See. I'm going to get this battery started." I pushed a shiny nail into one side of the lemon. It didn't puncture the skin until I jammed it in with a good shove. "It's coated in zinc." I waved a piece of wire. "My mom helped me cut a piece of this." I pushed it in easy peasy. "The wire is copper. You can also use an old penny. See, the zinc wants to wave bye-bye to the electrons. And the copper wants to collect them. When the electrons zip along—you get electricity. Which is going to power up this

35

little robot." I patted the lever-like arms.

From a nearby table Rory hooted, "Go robot power!" And I heard Birdie cheering, too.

Using alligator clips, I connected the zinc nail and copper wire to the place where the old battery had been in the robot.

"Let me zoom in on this," said Ms. Gottfried.

"All right," I said. "Ready, get set! Go!"

Nothing. The robot didn't budge.

"Maybe I put the positive side on the negative side," I said. "The red goes on the positive. And the black goes on the negative."

Avery whirled around from the table next to ours. "Do you have them on correctly?" She puckered her lips, which were blueberry blue from her lip gloss demo.

"I know I did the battery right." I gritted my teeth.

"You'll figure it out," said Elijah.

"I sure hope so," I murmured.

"I'm going to go over and take some photos of the other projects," said Ms. Gottfried.

"Okay." I smiled but inside I felt like such a fool. My cheeks warmed. "I can't believe it didn't work." Taking a deep breath, I tried to relax.

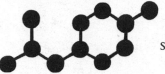

"Let's meet over by my desk," said Ms. Daly in a gentle voice.

I dragged over to Ms. Daly, whose desk was more like a counter in the front of the lab.

"Kate, what do you think happened?" she asked.

"Maybe it's a bad lemon. I read that before you stick in the copper and the zinc, you're supposed to squeeze the lemon. I forgot!"

"Okay," said Ms. Daly. "Did you think about how much power it takes to start a motor on a robot though?"

"No," I admitted. "I didn't even think about that. I should have probably tested how much power I needed."

"That's what I wanted to show you." Ms. Daly grabbed a small black machine off a shelf above her desk. "I have a voltmeter. We can test the voltage of your battery."

"That's awesome!" I had no idea that even existed. I wanted to borrow it and test the power of *everything*!

Ms. Daly placed the red probe tip on the copper. "Now you put the black probe tip on the zinc."

After I touched the black probe to the nail, the screen of the voltmeter read 0.912 V. "Probably not enough energy to power the robot," I said. "Is the V for volts?"

"Yup." Ms. Daly closed her eyes as if counting in her head. "If my math is correct, it would take over one thousand lemons to get that robot moving. You're going to need a lot more juice, if you want it to run."

I let out a low chuckle at Ms. Daly's corny joke. But inside, I was kicking myself for not thinking this through. I definitely needed to find something that used a lot less electricity than this robot. But what? My eyes scanned the items on Ms. Daly's desk. I spotted a simple-looking calculator. "Could I use that?"

"Of course," said Ms. Daly.

"Thank you so much." I waved the calculator in the air and called out to my group as I headed back to the table. "You guys, I'm going to use my lemons to fire up a calculator." I tried to sound happy but I was more than a weensy bit disappointed. A calculator was definitely not as cool as a robot. It might even be a little bit boring.

"I guess I really should have tested this"—I pointed to the lemon—"out first."

"You know what they say," said Jeremy. "It's always best to test."

"Who is *they*?" asked Phoenix.

Jeremy thumped his chest. "Me!" When he did that, my lemon knocked to the floor into a pile of sticky dirt that had fallen out of Phoenix's project earlier.

Groaning, I pulled the zinc and copper out of the lemon.

"When you get a lemon," I said, "sometimes you just have to make lemonade." Then I squashed the lemon under my foot, which felt good. I couldn't help feeling a little upset at the lemon, even though it wasn't its fault that it didn't generate enough juice to power the robot. Then I scooped up the lemon, wiped up its juice with my sleeve, and tossed it into the trash.

Phoenix's mouth dropped open. "Kate, why did you do that?" She pointed to the wastebasket. Then she took the lemon out again and added it to her composting project. At least the lemon would get to be part of STEM Night one way or another.

"Don't give up, Kate," said Ms. Daly from the next table, where she was helping Rory with his cloud experiment.

"I won't," I said, even though I wasn't feeling super excited about powering up a calculator. I thought about real scientists. Real scientists did not give up. They did not squash lemons. It took Thomas Edison over a thousand tries to invent the light bulb.

So I refused to be droopy about all of this. "It's okay, I have a bag of fresh lemons in the back. I'll get another one."

With the calculator in my hand, I raced to the side counter next to the sink where I had stored a bag of extra lemons. Only I didn't see the bag, so I checked the glass cabinet above. No bag. I checked again. I opened some drawers. Not there either. My eyes swept the counter surface, even the floor. But no luck. The lemons were gone!

CHAPTER EIGHT

MAKING LEMONADE

Materials (noun). An exact description of what is needed for a project or experiment. It should be clear enough that someone could copy your project. Think of it like a list of the ingredients in chocolate chip cookies. You can't leave anything out (especially not the chocolate chips!).

AFTER SCHOOL, I RACED TO THE FRIDGE to find more lemons. In one drawer, I dug through lettuce, carrots, and celery. In another, I found apples, pears, and even a persimmon.

"Not one? Really?" Outside, the clouds sat low and gray. It was beginning to drizzle. I hoped that didn't

mean soccer practice would be canceled. I so badly needed to kick a soccer ball right now. I paced in circles. Didn't Mom always have lemons around for her herbal tea? How could we be out? "I don't believe it."

Liam popped into the kitchen. "What don't you believe?"

"No lemons. And I need them for my science project."

"You need lemons so Norbert can do karate, right?" Liam chopped the air with his hands.

"I wish." Jumping up to sit on the counter, I swung my legs side to side. "I'm sorry. But I can't use your robot. Lemon batteries don't have enough power."

"Don't worry, Kate." Liam grunted and made muscles. His face turned as red as the maple tree in front of our house. "I got power for you!"

"You do. Lots." I laughed.

He started bouncing and spinning. And spinning some more.

"Have you been eating sugar?" I asked.

"Four grams," he said with a serious face.

"Where did you come up with that number?"

"Actually, I ate twenty hundred million grams.

My friend Gracie gave me a giant marshmallow." He motioned with his hands to show me.

"Oh, that explains everything."

He giggled. Then he got a serious look on his face. "Can't you go shopping for lemons? Maybe you could buy a whole lemon tree?"

I glanced at the clock on the microwave. "Avery's mom is picking me up in fifteen minutes. I've got soccer practice. At least, I hope I do. I'm worried the rain might make them cancel."

"Daddy and I can go shopping. He's finishing up some work in his office." Liam pointed to the kitchen doorway leading to Dad's home office. He's a psychologist.

"I heard my name," said Dad, striding into the kitchen. "How was school today?"

Oh boy. My dad isn't one for keeping your feelings to yourself. He encourages us to talk about pretty much everything. So I told him what happened today at school. All of it. Even the very embarrassing part.

"What a great experience," he said, smiling so his mustache waggled. "Realizing you made a miscalculation and that you need to try again."

"Great?" Maybe in Opposite Land. That's a land

that Birdie and I made up when we were little.

"All great scientists learn by what doesn't work," said Dad. "You know that."

"Yeah, I guess." That's when I told him about the missing lemons.

"Maybe they rolled onto the floor," suggested Dad.

"Or maybe somebody was hungry for lemonade." Liam mimed drinking.

"You mean thirsty." Dad ruffled Liam's hair.

"What's something else you know about science?" asked Dad. "Especially conclusions?"

"You don't jump to them," I said.

With a giggle, Liam jumped up onto a step stool. "Like this."

"Be careful, Liam." Dad pulled off his slippers and put on his running shoes.

"I have another problem." I pulled Ms. Daly's calculator out of my backpack. She said I could borrow it until STEM Night. "Powering it up doesn't seem like enough. I want to do something really cool that will impress the judges. Especially Dr. Caroline."

"Maybe you can add something special?" suggested Dad.

"Hot Wheels cars!" shouted Liam, making a vrooming sound. "With lots of jumps and ramps." Then he pointed to the stack of board games on our shelves. "It could crash into dominoes like in that Dr. Caroline video."

"Hey, that's a very interesting idea!" And that's when I remembered something high on the shelf right above my bed. "I'll be back in a sec!"

CHAPTER NINE

THe SWeet Spot

Matter (noun). Anything that takes up space, which means it has mass. It can be a solid, liquid, or gas. That means the air in a balloon is matter, the water that comes out of your kitchen sink is matter, and you're matter, too.

I PULLED A LARGE and very plump strawberry out of a wicker box on a shelf above my bed.

Liam charged into my bedroom. His eyes grew big. "Can I eat it? Yum!"

"Sorry, but it's not real."

"Aw, man." His little shoulders sagged. "It sure looks real."

"It's real in that it's made out

46

of matter. But you can't eat this strawberry because it's wax."

"Like a candle?" asked Liam regretfully.

"Yup! It was a birthday candle Birdie made for me, but it was so pretty I never asked Mom or Dad to light it." If it had been an actual strawberry, it would have decomposed like the orange in Phoenix's experiment. Luckily, it was art. Birdie gave it to me when I turned eight. She makes me something every year: a heart made out of yarn and Popsicle sticks, a hand-knitted scarf, a purple friendship bracelet. Each birthday present is awesome, and I kept all of them in my wicker box in my bedroom where Dribble, our dog, can't get to them.

But the wax strawberry might be the cutest. I loved the green stem and the little black wax seeds. "I can use this as part of my STEM project."

"Are you going to melt it?" asked Liam.

"No way." I shuddered, thinking about it all drippy and melty. "It's going to be part of my Rube Goldberg machine, just like in that Dr. Caroline video. Only I'm going to use lots of branches of science." My fingers brushed over the smooth cool surface of the strawberry. "Maybe the strawberry will plop into a cup and cause—"

"A flood?"

I laughed. "Something really awesome will definitely happen. You can count on it!"

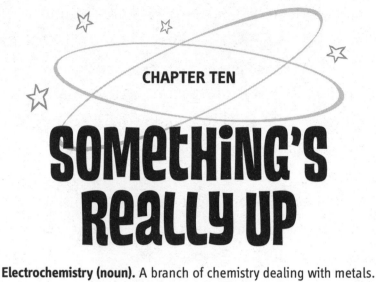

CHAPTER TEN

SOMETHING'S REALLY UP

Electrochemistry (noun). A branch of chemistry dealing with metals. An electrochemist figured out how to make the coating on your sunglasses and the microchip in your computer.

THE NEXT MORNING, Tuesday, I was skipping down the hall to class. Because last night, I had figured out my Rube Goldberg machine!

It was going to be so much fun to make. There was going to be stuff like a ramp, a pebble, dominoes, and Birdie's strawberry, of course!

Behind me, Elijah hurried to catch up.

"Wow. Kate," he called out. "You're in a rush."

"Yup!" I whirled around to wait for him. Then I explained to Elijah how I was going to put lemon batteries and the calculator into a Rube Goldberg machine. "I thought about it all last night. I'm going to use a few lemons to power a little fan, which is chemistry and engineering. Then blow a pebble down a ramp, which would be earth science and geology. The pebble will knock into dominoes, which is physics. And the dominoes will push the strawberry—which is botany, you know, the study of plants—off a ledge into a cup of water. The water will overflow, wetting a piece of tissue paper that's underneath it. Through capillary action (and more chemistry!), the spilled water will creep up the tissue paper that has been pulled tightly over a small vertical plastic arm. The water will force the tissue paper to break, and then the little plastic arm will pop up and push a button to turn on the vertically standing

calculator, which will also be powered by lemons!"

"So cool!" Elijah gushed. "It's kind of like a game we have at home—Mousetrap."

"That's just what Birdie said!" I had called her about the machine idea last night. "I just love that I'm getting so many branches of science into my demo. And I can explain all of them to Dr. Caroline. It's like I'm doing six projects in one!"

As I stood next to the water fountain, Rory slunk by and gave me a very strange look.

His eyebrows scrunched weirdly, as if I had my shirt on inside out or something. "What's with him?"

Elijah shrugged. "No clue."

"Well, I know what's up with *me*. I've got everything I need for my machine, including lemons, a ramp, dominoes, a cup, a wax strawberry, tissue paper, Ms. Daly's calculator, and a plastic arm." I twirled my grocery bag full of supplies. Then I whispered, "This time, I'm putting everything in the very back of my cubby in our classroom. That way nothing can fall out. And it would be harder for someone to grab."

"Do you think someone actually took the lemons yesterday? I mean, sure, if you wanted to make lemonade

But you'd need sugar, water, and a pitcher. What kid would have all of that?"

"Memito," I blurted.

"Oh, c'mon. Do you really think he would've done that?"

I thought about it. He loved anything to do with cooking and recipes. But I didn't think he would take my lemons. "Nah." I shook my head. "I don't think so." I looked both ways down the mostly empty hallway. We had driven in early with Mom. "I want to put the stuff back in the classroom without anybody seeing."

Elijah made a face. "So, I'm not anybody?"

"You're definitely somebody. You're one of my best friends. That's why you don't count as a suspect."

"Well, that's an acceptable answer," he said, and looked pleased.

He followed me into the classroom, where our teacher, Mrs. Eberlin, was stapling worksheets. "You two are in bright and early."

"Yes," I said. "Mom had an early meeting and we came with her. Plus, I wanted to put some of the materials for my STEM Night project away. To keep them safe."

"Good idea. How's the project going?" asked Mrs. Eberlin.

"Great," I said. And it was true. I was going in a different direction. But it felt so right.

Mrs. Eberlin neatened her stack. "How about you, Elijah?"

"Good." He pulled his drumsticks out of his backpack. "Getting graded to drum. Can't complain."

"It's always better to do what's in your heart," Mrs. Eberlin said with a smile.

Luckily for me, I loved science—all of it. And I loved that even with the Rube Goldberg machine, I was still doing some chemistry. Learning about how electrons move through metals was a branch of chemistry called electrochemistry. After gently stuffing all of my supplies, including the strawberry, in the back of my cubby, I turned to Elijah.

"I'm going to meet up with Birdie by the basketball court. Want to come?"

"Sure," said Elijah.

"See you soon," said Mrs. Eberlin.

All morning, all I could think about was my project. School dragged except for when we got to language arts.

That was because we were going to write haiku poems about our STEM project.

"And you get to write them with these," said Mrs. Eberlin, shaking a cardboard box mailer. "My sister Lucia mailed me pens from Buenos Aires."

"Yay!" cried Birdie.

Mrs. Eberlin held up different kinds and different colors. "My sister owns an art supply store. And these are some extra mismatched ones that she had lying around. They're a present for doing such good work so far on your language arts projects. Just reach on in there and pick which pen you'd like."

Birdie picked a cyan blue one.

I picked a fuchsia pink one.

Then we used the pens to write haiku about our science projects.

A haiku is a type of Japanese poetry that I love because it's so organized. The first line has five syllables, the second line seven, and the last line has five.

"You know why I like haiku?" said Elijah. "Because they're short poems."

"Don't you like poetry?" asked Phoenix.

"I do, but I like it even better when it's short," he said.

"It definitely makes it faster to write," I added as I finished my own poem.

Rube Goldberg Machine

    By Kate Crawford

This cool machine is

A chain reaction that shows

Six types of science

Mrs. Eberlin loved our poems and said she was going to put them up on the class bulletin board. And best of all, after language arts, it was finally time for us to bring our materials to the science lab.

Racing over to my cubby, I grabbed the bag of supplies. Then I carefully pulled out the tissue-wrapped wax strawberry.

I called Birdie over. "Your present is going to be the most important part of my Rube Goldberg machine," I said, my voice rising in excitement. "It will be awesome."

"Let me see."

I slowly unwrapped Birdie's strawberry.

Only it didn't look like a strawberry.

It was completely smooshed. "What?!" I stared at

the misshapen glob of wax. "How did this happen? I wrapped it extra carefully."

I blinked my eyes really quickly so I wouldn't cry.

Birdie put her arm on my shoulder. "It's okay, Kate. I can warm it up and reshape it. It's a special modeling kind of beeswax. That strawberry will be fine."

"Thanks, Birdie. You're the best, really. But . . . do you think someone is messing with my stuff on purpose?" Feeling unsteady, I walked up to my teacher and told her what happened.

"I'm sorry, Kate," she said. "But I didn't see anyone go near your cubby. And I've been in the classroom all day. Except for during my lunch and part of my planning period."

"So, it could have happened then," I said.

"I don't think so," she said. "Someone would have to be awfully sneaky. Maybe when you stuffed it into the cubby you accidentally smushed it a bit."

"Maybe," I said. But I didn't think so. I had been so careful. Plus, this came after the missing lemons. I might have been able to shrug off one mystery, but two? This seemed deliberate.

During science lab, I could barely concentrate on

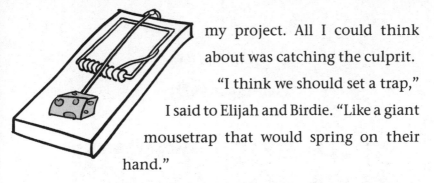

my project. All I could think about was catching the culprit.

"I think we should set a trap," I said to Elijah and Birdie. "Like a giant mousetrap that would spring on their hand."

"They would be caught red-handed, that's for sure," said Elijah.

"You guys," said Birdie. "I don't think setting a trap is a very good idea. Don't you think this person would see it? I mean, if it were big and all?"

"I know," I said. "Maybe we could convince Mrs. Eberlin to install a hidden camera in the classroom. And we could get video footage."

"Then we'd have to watch hours of your cubby," said Birdie.

"It might not be so bad," said Elijah. "Sometimes on YouTube my mom watches this channel that's just a video of a babbling stream. It's called the Calm Channel."

"I don't think watching Kate's cubby would be calm." Birdie let out an exasperated sigh.

"It's okay," I said. "I'll figure out some other way to catch the culprit."

CHAPTER ELEVEN

A Strawberry ON TOP

Heat (noun). From a chemistry standpoint, heat is energy flowing from a hotter system to a cooler one. If you give off energy, things heat up. If you take it away, things cool down. That's why if you do a hundred jumping jacks, you'll start to sweat.

"I HAVE SOMETHING FOR YOU," said Birdie on Friday at lunch.

"What?" I asked. We sat in the cafeteria away from

everyone, behind the wilty salad bar.

Normally, we sat at a long table in a big group. But

I wanted a little chance to relax. It still felt like someone was out to get me. And I had no idea who or why.

Birdie held out a white paper bag.

I pressed my hands together. "Please, Birdie. You know I have zero patience. Tell me what's in there. I'm begging you!"

"Close your eyes and count to ten."

"Okay, fine." I squeezed my eyes shut. And started to count. "One Michigan," I began. "Two Michigan."

I could hear Birdie opening the bag.

"Three Michigan."

The sound of more paper crinkling.

"Four Michigan. I can't stand it. Five, six, seven, eight, nine-ten," I rushed, then fluttered my eyes open.

And there sitting on top of Birdie's palm was my strawberry candle.

It looked just like it had before. Only better, if that was possible. "That looks amazing. So real. I mean, I actually want to eat it."

"You think it's your wax strawberry. It's a real one," she said with a serious voice.

"Really?"

"Just kidding. But it does look real, doesn't it?"

"Yes," I admitted. "I could almost forget that it was ever messed up. Like maybe it was just a figment of my imagination."

"It wasn't your imagination," said Birdie firmly. "It looked like someone warmed it up in their hands and then squeezed it really hard to smash it." Birdie bit into her taco. "I just don't get who would do something like that."

"Me either. Maybe it was a hungry rat who was confused."

"Ha ha. That's weird."

"What's weird is the way Rory is looking over at me." I nodded over to the table where he sat with Elijah and a bunch of guys. Rory peered at me again and then looked away when I tried to catch his eye. Then he whispered to Memito.

"Okay. That is weird," whispered Birdie.

"I know." At that moment, as if Rory knew we were talking about him, he snuck a glance at me one more time. I gave him a questioning look and he whipped around.

"Weirder," I said.

"Agreed," said Birdie, dipping her spoon in some rice pudding, which was dusted with cocoa powder.

"Hold up! That's cocoa powder."

"Yummy. And pretty."

"And also, a great tool." I remembered a Dr. Caroline episode about dusting for fingerprints with cocoa powder. I explained how it worked to Birdie and then I zipped to the lunch counter. Mrs. Andrews, who manages the cafeteria, was sealing the lid on a jar of mayonnaise.

"Can I please have some cocoa powder? Just a small cup. It's for a really good reason. A science experiment."

"Science, huh?" She looked at me. She looked over at a plastic container of cocoa. "I don't see why not. Is it for class, Kate, or are you doing something on your own? Your mom told me about your kitchen science experiments earlier this week."

I smiled at her. It's always a little weird that the grown-ups at school know things about me that I didn't tell them. But sometimes it's kind of nice, too.

"There's a science project competition, one week from this Friday." I pointed to a banner in the cafeteria that read: STEM NIGHT! NOV. 20!

"Oh right!" She measured out a cup and handed it to me in a baggie. "Good luck!"

"Thanks." Back at the table, I turned to Birdie.

"Sometimes having your mom as principal has some perks." As fast as we could, we went to Mrs. Eberlin's classroom, which was always open to students at lunch.

We said hi to Mrs. Eberlin, who stood in the middle of the classroom with a stack of books in her arms.

"What are you girls up to?" she asked as she strolled toward the back of the classroom.

"Oh, just a little science," I said, which was the truth.

"Well, have fun, girls. I'm going to do a little reshelving." She disappeared behind a bookshelf area we call the book nook. "Holler if you need anything."

"We will," I said.

Explaining the procedure to Birdie, I quickly gathered everything we needed (luckily Birdie always has art supplies in her backpack and it was cold enough out that we had gloves in our jacket pockets):

2 pairs of gloves—to avoid putting our prints all over everything, or getting cocoa powder all over us

1 tablespoon of cocoa powder—not to make hot chocolate but to dust for fingerprints

1 paintbrush with soft bristles—to apply the cocoa powder, not for a Birdie masterpiece

1 roll of tape—not to tape stuff together but to lift off the fingerprints

1 index card—to stick the lifted fingerprint to for evidence

Birdie pulled on a pair of purple gloves that she'd bedazzled with rhinestones. "My prints will not be contaminating the evidence."

"Definitely not." I grabbed some of the cocoa powder and poured it into my cubby. Then I picked up the paintbrush.

"How does it actually work?" asked Birdie.

"Fingers are coated with sweat and oil. That means the powder will stick to it. Dark powder works best on a light surface." After lightly swishing the brush back and forth, I gently blew away the excess powder. "Look!" I pointed to three fingerprints.

"Wow," whispered Birdie.

"I know."

Birdie cut off three strips of tape. "It's time for lift-off." Smoothing the strips over the prints, she pulled them off the surface of the cubby. Then she stuck the pieces of tape to the index card.

Voila! We definitely had three perfect-looking prints.

But I realized there were two problems:

1) I had no idea if the prints were mine or someone else's.

2) If they were someone else's, I didn't have access to a fingerprint database.

Luckily, I could take care of the first problem at home. The second one had me stumped.

CHAPTER TWELVE

FOCUSING ON THE POSITIVE

Positive charge (noun). When an atom is missing an electron or two, it will have a positive charge. It's like having a balance scale with a pound of lollipops on one side and a pound of chocolate on the other. If you take away a lollipop, you'll now have more chocolate than lollipops.

AFTER SCHOOL, Elijah passed the soccer ball to me and I drove it down the field. The wind blew against my face. It was chilly outside, but I didn't mind.

Running with the ball felt good, almost easy.

If only my science project felt

that way, too. If only I could figure out who was messing with me.

"You got this!" cheered Elijah.

"Go, Kate!" shouted Avery, waving at me from the opposite side of the field. Streams of sunlight broke through the clouds.

I got this, I told myself.

But I wasn't so sure. Rory stood in my way. I mean, he literally stood. He wasn't coming at me. But more like standing still waving his arms, trying to intimidate me. On my team, I'm a defender, so I'm not as confident when it comes to duking it out. But I was going to have to speed past him. He was my obstacle. *Calm down*, I told myself. *This isn't a real game.*

It was just a pickup game after school.

Tapping the ball to the side, I used a quick change of direction to scoot past him. Yes! I dribbled down the field. The goal was getting closer. Just as Jeremy tried to take possession, I kicked. The ball lifted off, arcing into the air and into the goal.

"Oh yeah," I cried, racing to grab the ball before I booted it back to midfield for the kickoff.

Elijah high-fived me. Avery yelled "Goal!" and I saw

the sunlight reflect off her sparkly red lip gloss, the latest color from her STEM project.

"Hold up," said Jeremy. "Are you actually saying that was a goal?"

"Uh-huh!" I said. "It went right between the goal post markers."

"Dude, it did," said Elijah. "I placed the rocks exactly where we always put the cones."

Jeremy folded his arms in front of his chest. He peered at Rory. "You were closer than me. Did you see it go between those rocks?"

Rory stared at me. He looked at Jeremy and then he considered the goal. "Um, yeah. Sort of. I did."

"Sorry. I couldn't see it," said Jeremy. "This is why this school needs soccer nets!"

"They would be helpful," said Rory.

Jeremy waved his arms emphatically. "We should have them. It's basic equipment. If you win the STEM competition, you should also use the money to buy goals," Jeremy said to Rory.

Rory peered back toward the school. "Actually, I want to buy more books for the library. I've read every science fiction series in there."

"Me too," I agreed. "I love sci-fi."

"Cool," said Rory. "Uh, Kate, looks like your mom wants you." Following his gaze, I spotted Mom, standing with Liam on the blacktop. She signaled it was time for us to go.

"Okay, see you tomorrow, everyone," I called out.

"Don't count this as a win because we didn't finish," Jeremy called after me.

"Sure." I jogged backward. "It doesn't matter, anyway. We'll beat you tomorrow, too."

"You wish!" shouted Jeremy.

Elijah caught up to me. "Man, Jeremy is as competitive as you are."

"Yeah," I admitted. "I definitely like to win." Winning made me think of the STEM competition, which had been in my brain almost nonstop. I bit my lip and turned to Elijah. "I'm not sure I'm going to do so hot on the STEM competition, especially with someone sabotaging me. I just wish I knew who it was. Then I could stop them!"

"Focus on the positive," suggested Elijah.

"Hmm. When I think of the positive, I think of a positive charge, which makes me think of my project, which makes me get worried all over again." With a sigh, I folded my arms across my chest.

"C'mon, Kate. Just think about what you'll do with the money."

"I don't know," I mumbled.

"How about buying more test tubes? Or lights and lasers for a musical talent show."

"Maybe. But I want it to be . . . you know, something that feels essential."

Everyone except me seemed to have great ways to spend the prize money. But it wouldn't even matter if I didn't figure out what was going on with my project. I'd never win if someone kept messing with my stuff.

I tapped my pocket, which had the index card of fingerprints inside. Hopefully that would lead me to the answer.

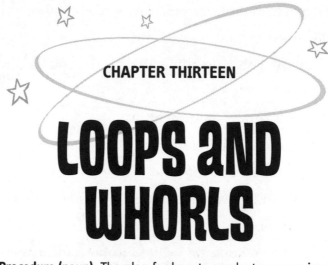

CHAPTER THIRTEEN

LOOPS AND WHORLS

Procedure (noun). The plan for how to conduct an experiment or demonstration. Think of it like a recipe for baking cupcakes. If you fail to follow a step (like adding the sugar), it won't turn out very well.

"LIAM, DO YOU WANT TO PLAY detective?" My brother and I munched on granola bars at the kitchen table after school.

"Can I be a superhero and a detective?" he asked, popping the last bite of bar into his mouth.

"Sure, why not—you can be a detective-superhero."

"Yes!" He zipped out of the kitchen. Five minutes

later, he reappeared in his Batman pajama top with the cape attached.

"You look ready!" I exclaimed.

I showed him the fingerprint I had collected from my cubby. Then I explained how we were looking for a culprit based on a match. But that we had to identify my own print first to make sure the ones I collected weren't mine.

"So, the first thing I'm going to do is get my prints." I pushed my thumb down into a pad of blue ink and then pressed it onto a white piece of paper. Then I did the same thing with the rest of my fingers. "Tada! Those are all my fingerprints. And it's the first step in our procedure." Then I wrote my name in big block letters under the print.

"I want to do it too." Liam rolled his thumb and his other fingers into the inkpad almost at once. "Tada!" he shouted. Grabbing a red crayon, he wrote his name in huge letters so that there wasn't room for the M in Liam. Flipping his paper over, he wrote a giant M on the other side.

I pointed to our prints. "See how they're different? See the pattern of the loops and whorls?"

He studied his thumbprint. "It looks like a little hill." Then he examined mine. "Your center swirl is crooked. I want mine to be crooked too."

"Sorry, buddy. Can't help you. That's the thing about fingerprints. Every single person has a different one. Even twins."

"Hey, that's like snowflakes. Ms. Chen taught us about that. Each one is unique." Ms. Chen is Liam's kindergarten teacher. She has a special handshake for each of her students. And Liam thinks she's the coolest.

"Your fingerprint patterns are formed before you were even born," I explained.

"When I was in Mommy's tummy?"

"Yup. Basically, we leave behind fingerprints all the time. On doorknobs, glasses, tables. But we can't always see them with the naked eye."

He pointed to his eyes. "Unless you got x-ray vision. Like me—superhero detective boy."

"True," I said. "Okay, now is the moment of truth. We're going to see if there's a match. Or whether someone else has had their hands in my cubby. It's showtime!" If Elijah were here, he'd do a drumroll.

My heart fluttered in anticipation.

I compared the prints to mine. Also to Liam's, because why not.

Nothing matched up.

They were completely different prints. All three of them were. Two looked like maybe pointer fingers and one was definitely a thumb.

"It's confirmed!" There was someone sabotaging me. Now there was just one problem. I didn't know how to figure out who it could be.

CHAPTER FOURTEEN

A VOLT AND A JOLT

Volt (noun). A unit used when measuring the amount of electricity in a battery. Something small like a remote control needs a few volts of electricity, but a remote-controlled car needs a LOT more.

IT WAS THREE DAYS before STEM Night. On Tuesday afternoon, we were in the science lab, getting time for our projects with Ms. Daly. Like always, we had to work at a table with our assigned groups.

"Okay, everyone, my Rube Goldberg machine is going to turn on that calculator." I pointed to the calculator that Ms. Daly had given me.

"I'm ready to watch this," said Memito.

"Me too," said Jeremy.

"Me three," said Phoenix.

The first thing I did was to power my very low-volt, handheld fan with a battery made from six lemons. This time I had remembered to roll the fresh lemons to soften up the insides before making my batteries. And to test them using the voltmeter.

Now came the moment to see if my concept for the machine would work. I used blocks to prop up an upside-down lunch tray to the exact height of my little fan. Then I placed a small round pebble at the beginning of a Hot Wheels track on top of the tray. Then at the end of the track, I stacked six dominoes in a row. There was just enough space to carefully balance Birdie's strawberry between the last domino and the very edge of the tray. Below the tray, I set a glass full of water.

"Okay, ready?" I cried. "One, two, three, go!"

After I turned on the fan, it powered the pebble, which rolled down the track to knock into the dominoes, which pushed the strawberry off the lunch tray into the cup of water with a satisfying plop. The water overflowed, wetting the piece of tissue paper underneath it.

"Cool!" cried Phoenix.

"Yeah," admitted Jeremy. "That's like something you'd see on YouTube."

"But you didn't get the calculator to turn on." Memito shook his head. "Oh, man, that's not good."

"It's fine!" I said. "I haven't finished building my machine." I pointed to my bag. "I've got more tissue paper in here and a little plastic arm. All I have to do is strap down the arm using tightly pulled tissue paper. When the cup overflows, the tissue paper will get all soggy, releasing the arm, which will spring up to hit the on button on the calculator. Plus, I'm also going to power up the calculator with these." I pulled out two more lemons. "Tada!"

"Mmmm, those smell good," sniffed Phoenix.

"Maybe I could make fruit leather out of them," said Memito.

"No," I said. "Like I told you. I need them to make another battery."

"It's time for a milk break, everyone." Jeremy held up a half quart each of chocolate and strawberry milk. On his tray were half quarts of fat-free and low-fat milk.

"Oh, strawberry is my favorite. I'll take that," said

Memito, grabbing the carton of strawberry milk.

Jeremy yanked it away from Memito. "Dude, that's part of my experiment. To see what happens when you pour Red Bull in the milk." He popped open a can of Red Bull. "The acid in this stuff will curdle milk. At least that's what I'm hoping. And I want to see which kind of milk curdles the most."

Phoenix made a face. "Think what it will do to your stomach."

Jeremy poured different kinds of milk in four empty flasks. Then he topped them off with Red Bull.

The strawberry milk immediately separated. On the top it was foaming. With the chocolate milk you couldn't see the separation as much but you could tell something was going on. After  a few more minutes, the low-fat milk and fat-free milk got clumpy.

Meanwhile, Memito was taking photos. *Click. Click. Click.*

"Okay, you're going to want to get this!" Jeremy

dumped the low-fat milk and the fat-free milk into the sink. There were clumps of curdled milk that looked like cottage cheese. "Say cheese!" cried Jeremy.

Memito held his nose. "Wow, that reeks."

"Keep taking photos," said Jeremy. The strawberry milk and the chocolate milk barely came out of the flask. "It's not budging." Finally, giant clumps plopped out.

Memito put down the camera.

"Take another photo!" urged Jeremy. "You can't miss this."

"Okay, I won't breathe," joked Memito, who took a few more shots.

"That was pretty stinky," I admitted. "But I've got to go. Not because of the stink—well, a little bit because of it."

"You don't know what you're missing," said Jeremy.

"I'm going to get my poster board," I said. "To add to the observations section."

I hurried to the back of the lab. But when I went to look at my poster board, I couldn't believe what was scribbled right under my drawing of my Rube Goldberg machine.

CHAPTER FIFTEEN

STARTING FROM SQUARE ONE

Voltmeter (noun). A special instrument that measures how much electricity is passing between two points. But it sounds like it should be an instrument that measures the badness in the Harry Potter bad guy Volt-emort.

I BLINKED A FEW TIMES to make sure I wasn't imagining anything.

When I opened my eyes, it was still there. And I was furious.

Someone had taken a pen and written on my poster board. *Kate is bad at science.*

I started to shake. Immediately, Birdie zipped over

to me. "Look," I said. "See what somebody did!"

"I'm so sorry, Kate. That's just not right."

"I can't believe someone would mess with my project like this. And write something so untrue. First of all, I am NOT bad at science!"

"Kate, science is your life. It's how your brain operates. This person is living in Opposite Land."

"Thank you," I said. "Because lately with my project off to a slow start, I've been having doubts."

"That's natural. Everyone feels that way. There are days I feel like I can't draw. At all. Like I should give up."

"You're too hard on yourself."

"Ditto," she said. And we both sort of smiled. Because we ditto each other a lot.

"How am I going to redo all the work I did on my poster? It took me hours to draw that lemon using a light board. I can't do it again." I looked over at the volunteer moms helping out at the front of the classroom. "Plus, I don't want to explain to those moms why I need a new piece of poster board. It would be embarrassing."

"You didn't do anything. Someone else did."

"Yeah, but they might think I did something to deserve it." Tears welled up behind my eyes. My throat puckered like I had just swallowed one of my own lemons. "And what if they tell my mom . . ."

"It's going to be okay," said Birdie in a soothing voice.

"I'm not so sure."

"You can fix this. Just draw a box around the writing and color it in with black marker. You used a voltmeter to test the lemons, right? So you turn the box into a voltmeter. A nice big square. See?" On a piece of paper, she took a pencil and sketched a box.

"Oh, you're right. That might actually look good."

I studied her paper. "I wish I had your artistic talent. But since I don't, I'm glad you're around to show me how to deal with this. I just want to catch that person messing with me."

Suddenly Birdie went quiet. "Kate," she whispered. "I think I know how we can catch them!"

CHAPTER SIXTEEN

SPILLED INK

Chromatography (noun). A way of separating a mixture of molecules. It's like a bunch of kids racing. At first, they're all jumbled up but soon they spread out, as faster kids take the lead.

BIRDIE GRABBED MY POSTER BOARD, the one with the writing on it that said: *Kate is bad at science.*

From her supply box, she snagged scissors.

"What are you doing?" I cried.

"I'm going to cut off a letter."

"But that's going to mess it up." I bit my lip.

"Kate, trust me. In order to get evidence, I need to cut. You can tape a piece of paper underneath and no one will know the difference."

"Okay, okay," I said, hiding my eyes. "But I can't look."

The scissors went *snip snip*. And then I peeked. Birdie had cut off a strip of the poster board with the letter *K* on it. "I'm getting a sample," she said. "To do some chromatography."

"Oooooh, now I get it." When you see blue ink—it's way more than just blue. It's got a whole bunch of colors swirled together to make that particular shade. Chromatography gives you a way to separate out all of those colors. And for detective work, it's awesome since each different kind of ink is going to have a different mix of color.

"Now, we know that the culprit used some kind of blue pen," said Birdie. "But since Mrs. Eberlin gave out all different kinds of pens, this blue ink is going to be unique. Since no pen was the same, no ink will look the same once we separate it."

"Just like a fingerprint," I said with growing excitement.

"Exactly." Birdie grabbed a beaker and filled it with water. Then she taped the strip with the *K* to a pencil. It

dangled like a little flag. "Watch," she said. "The water is a solvent. It's going to dissolve the ink and then it will spread across the paper." She hung the pencil over the top of the beaker so that the bottom of the strip barely touched the water. As the water soaked up into the paper, the ink spread upward.

Biting my lip, I glanced over at the large strips of tissue paper hanging on Birdie's poster board.

The blue ink had spread upward but was no longer blue. It was pinkish at the bottom and light blue where ink bloomed upward. "Whoever thought a crime could look so pretty." I bent to inspect. "Now we need to test our suspects."

Fifteen minutes later, we were back in Mrs. Eberlin's room for free read, where Birdie and I usually flop down in the beanbag chairs with our books. Instead, Birdie dragged me to the bulletin board and pointed to four different haiku poems written in blue pen. "I just need to steal those poems off the wall and test them!"

"Keep it down. We'll get in so

much trouble!" I looked for Mrs. Eberlin. She was going over some writing with Avery up at her desk. Today, Avery's lips were a sparkly lime green.

Birdie shrugged. "We don't have any other choice. Unless you want to go tell Mrs. Eberlin."

I shook my head. "No way. If I tell her, she'll tell Mom. And then it *will* be a big deal. Everyone will talk about how the principal's daughter is getting bullied. We've got to figure this out ourselves." Being a principal's daughter has its perks, but it also has its downsides.

"We'll just have to figure out some way to get the poems when nobody is looking," whispered Birdie. "Maybe after school?"

I studied the bylines on the blue poems on the bulletin board: Avery, Jeremy, Elijah, and Rory. "We'll have to keep our eyes on them," I said. "Every one of them is a suspect."

"Even Elijah?" Birdie asked.

I gulped. "Even Elijah," Even though I didn't think that Elijah really could have done it. But he *was* the only one who saw me put the strawberry in my cubby . . . I had to be sure.

CHAPTER SEVENTEEN

SeeKiNG SOLUtiONS

Erlenmeyer flask (noun). A container with slanted sides and a narrow neck named after the chemist Emil Erlenmeyer. Since they're often made of special material that doesn't break under heat, you could easily make hot chocolate in one over the stove.

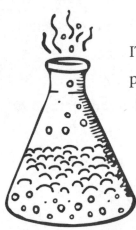

IT WAS WEDNESDAY, and a day had passed since Birdie had figured out how to solve the mystery. Now there were more and more volunteer parents helping out in the classroom because STEM Night was just two days away. How could we find an

opportunity to test our samples without getting caught?

It seemed impossible.

Inside the classroom, my eyes scanned the poems on the bulletin board for the hundredth time.

Specifically, the poems in blue written by the suspects: Avery, Jeremy, Elijah, and Rory.

"Is everything okay, Kate?" asked Mrs. Eberlin.

"Yes, it's fine. I'm just thinking."

"About your STEM project, I bet."

"I was." Although more about how to catch a culprit messing up my project.

"Well, I was glad to see that your squashed strawberry got fixed," she said. "Luckily"—she glanced up at the clock—it's lunchtime. If you want to get in some extra minutes for your project, you can eat your lunch in the lab. Ms. Daly will be there."

Normally, I would jump at that offer. But for the first time ever, I didn't want to go to the lab.

Instead, I wanted to stay behind and test the ink. But for now, that didn't seem like it was going to happen. Mrs. Eberlin usually ate her lunch at her desk. So I left the room to meet Birdie in the cafeteria.

After I gobbled down my ham sandwich, I headed to

the lab with Birdie to work on finishing up my poster. I had all of my materials. And my explanation on how my Rube Goldberg machine worked was almost done. I was proud of the fact that my demonstration would touch on engineering, physics, earth science, geology, botany, and, of course, chemistry. *Six* sciences total. "Your strawberry makes the machine seem extra yummy," I said.

"I think Dr. Caroline will love it," said Birdie.

"She's going to love yours too."

"Maybe." Birdie sighed. "But the tissue paper keeps tearing. It's not going to look good."

"Why don't you use a coffee filter instead?" I pulled out a bunch of filters from my bag. "I tried it out for my Rube Goldberg machine and it was too strong when it got wet. The little arm wouldn't pop up to hit the calculator. But it would be perfect for you. Filters are pretty tough." I pulled on one to demonstrate.

Birdie's eyes brightened. "That's a great idea, Kate. Thanks so much."

"No, thank you," I said.

"No, thank you."

And then we got into a huge thank-you contest and burst out laughing.

That's when Memito and Jeremy strolled into the lab. Memito stopped in front of my poster. "Hey, what are you laughing about?" he asked.

Birdie and I looked at each other. "You sort of had to be there," I said, grabbing the strawberry.

"Hey, that looks so real." He patted his stomach. "Luckily, I just ate my lunch. Otherwise, I'd be hungry."

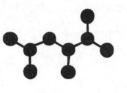 "Luckily, your project happens to be fruit leather," said Birdie.

Memito smacked his lips. "On STEM Night, a taste of my delicious fruit leather will make people hungry for more. You better hope nobody tries to eat that strawberry."

Or smashes it, I thought. But I didn't say anything.

"Kate shouldn't even be allowed to use that." Jeremy pointed to my calculator. "Because it's a teacher's."

"That's ridiculous," I said. "What about your project? You borrowed flasks from the classroom."

"That's different." Jeremy folded his arms. "Those are classroom ones for the science lab. Yours is Ms. Daly's personal calculator."

From halfway across the room, Avery pressed her lips together. Today, they were peach colored. "I saw the calculator come off of Ms. Daly's desk too," she said.

"Yes, but a calculator is for educational purposes." I studied the flasks. "I don't see the difference between your flasks and my calculator. They're both being borrowed. Anyway, the point is—I made two actual batteries with lemons!"

Avery waved her little tin of lip gloss. "So far my peach gloss has stayed on for forty-two minutes, just as long as the store-bought one. Can't wait to see how much longer it lasts. But either way, it looks great."

Phoenix smiled at Avery. "It really does."

"And it isn't made of bad chemicals." Avery smacked her lips. "I think I'm going to win because Dr. Caroline and Mrs. Eberlin both wear lipstick."

"Ms. Daly doesn't," I pointed out. "Anyway, lip gloss and lipstick aren't the same."

Avery shrugged. "I'm sure the other judges will outvote Ms. Daly." She tilted her neck as if someone were taking a photo of her. "I'm going to use the prize to get new curtains for the theater." She looked at me expectantly. "What will you do if you win?" She said it like I couldn't possibly come up with anything good.

"Maybe we should upgrade the science lab?" I

realized that my voice lifted in a question. I was still unsure. And that really bugged me.

"Are you saying our lab isn't good enough?" asked Avery, loud enough for Ms. Daly, who was in the back of the classroom organizing equipment for STEM Night, to hear.

"I didn't mean it like that." I could feel my cheeks turning pink. I felt bad about even the possibility of hurting Ms. Daly.

And then it hit me. Avery sounded really upset. Could she be the one who was sabotaging my stuff?

CHAPTER EIGHTEEN

ALMOST SHOWTIME!

Scientific testing (noun). The process of investigating hypotheses. It is one of the most important jobs of a scientist. Kind of like the most important job of a professional skateboarder is to practice tricks and stunts.

ANOTHER DAY HAD PASSED without a single opportunity to test the ink. At least nobody had tried to mess with my project again. Which was good since STEM Night was tomorrow. I couldn't believe it! Yesterday, I had made sure to be the last person out of the science lab before Ms. Daly locked it up. I wasn't taking any chances.

In class, Mrs. Eberlin had reminded us to finish up

our poster boards. When everyone started chatting about STEM Night during free time, I studied Elijah for signs of dishonesty. His arms hung loosely at his sides. His jaw was relaxed. But his eyes focused on his notebook. Not once did he look at me directly.

Did this mean that Elijah was feeling guilty about something? Like, maybe, messing up my project?

It didn't seem possible.

But in science you can't close your mind to possibilities. You don't know unless you test something. I just had to test the ink in those poems.

I headed over to the pencil sharpener in the back of the class. As I did, Rory gave me a strange look. Like he knew I was up to something. I ended up grinding my pencil way too much. I groaned.

The bell blared. Everyone gabbed away as they cleared off their desks to go to recess. "Finally," said Memito, who was my desk partner.

Kids lined up at the door and then took off.

I was about to zip out the

door, too, when Mrs. Eberlin said, "I can't believe STEM Night is coming right up."

"Tomorrow," I said.

Mrs. Eberlin peered up at the calendar on the wall. She wrinkled her freckled nose. "Please tell me how that happened."

"I don't know," Birdie said, walking over to join me. "I guess when you're working on science, time flies."

"Or as Ms. Daly would say," I added, "time flies like an arrow. Fruit flies like a banana." We all laughed. Because it was one of Ms. Daly's favorite jokes.

"Speaking of flying," Mrs. Eberlin said, "I've got to get going on the magnet station I'm in charge of for STEM Night."

She brushed past the social studies center and the reading corner. Then she disappeared into the walk-in supply closet at the very back of the room. "Wish me luck!" she called out. "I might be in here a while!"

I flicked a glance at Birdie. We could stay in the classroom and take off enough ink from each poem to do some testing.

Birdie looked at me, reading my mind.

"Now?" she asked under her breath.

"Yes," I whispered back.

Birdie slunk over to the bulletin board. My fingers quickly tugged along the edge of a poem until I found the thumbtack.

I pulled one out when Birdie waved her hands frantically. "She's coming back."

My fingers flew off the board just as Mrs. Eberlin popped back over. She looked at us funny. "What are you girls still doing in here? Shouldn't you already be outside?"

I shrugged. "Forgot my coat." The lie felt sharp and hot on my tongue.

"That's not like you, Kate."

I shrugged sheepishly. No. It wasn't. First of all, I don't usually forget things. And second of all, I don't lie. "My mind is on my project," I said, and that part was true.

"Well, go outside and have some fun," said Mrs. Eberlin. "It's never this nice this time of year."

But I wasn't so sure I could have fun. After all, she came back so quickly that I wasn't able to get a single poem off the board.

I had more sleuthing to do.

CHAPTER NINETEEN

PARTNERS IN CRIME

Vinegar (noun). An acid that is used in many science experiments. It's also good to use as an ingredient for salad dressing, but you wouldn't want to drink it by itself!

"LET'S NOT THINK ABOUT TOMORROW," said Birdie as she swung on the monkey bars. "You've got to give yourself a break, Kate."

Outside, the sun was shining. It was almost warm enough to shed my coat.

"You're right," I said, trying not to think about all of the sabotage.

"Let's have a hanging upside down contest."

"You'll win."

She laughed. "You don't know that. Hey, look, Kate."
She pointed to the clouds. "Doesn't it look like a giant question mark? It's like the sky is curious."

"Cool!" Birdie always saw things differently than me. Maybe that's what made her a great artist.

Grabbing a bar, I started to swing when I noticed Rory whispering with Elijah. They were friends, so that part wasn't weird. What was weird was that they kept on staring at me like maybe I was a baking soda and vinegar volcano that was about to explode.

I continued to swing on the monkey bars, but I could feel their stares burning into the back of my head.

"That's it!" I dropped down on the ground with a hard thump.

Birdie glanced at me confused. "What's *it*?"

"I'll tell you in a minute." I stormed over to Elijah as he headed toward the line to play tetherball. "What's

97

going on? Why were you and Rory just looking at me? It was weird."

Elijah kept on walking on the field. "No reason." A group of shrieking third graders playing tag brushed past us.

"There was a reason. Tell me. Plus, this isn't the first time that Rory has been giving me weird looks."

Elijah stopped. He seemed reluctant to turn around. "Can't say," he whispered.

My hands pressed against my mouth. It all became clear as a crystal.

"You and Rory are trying to sabotage my project," I stated hotly.

Elijah squinted painfully as if he were staring into direct sunlight. Only the sun had just gone behind some clouds. "Well, well . . . you see—"

"I caught you! Ha!"

Elijah tugged nervously on his hair. "Kate. Don't be mad. Please. It's not what you think. I'd never mess with your project." He looked so sincere. "You've got to believe me." His voice quavered as if he were really upset. "That's not what it is at all."

"So, it's Rory, then. You're protecting him. I knew it!'

Elijah sighed. "Not about that. It's . . . Rory's mom is letting him have a boy/girl party for his birthday. And he wanted to invite you. And he was asking me if I thought you'd come."

It was all about a party? The tight knot of upset started to soften. "So, it's not Rory trying to ruin my project?"

He shook his head. "I don't think so."

I was quiet for a second and then I said, softly. "I'd come. If Rory invited me. You can . . . you can tell him that."

Then I walked back to Birdie.

So, it wasn't Elijah. And it wasn't Rory. That just left two people—Jeremy and Avery.

CHAPTER TWENTY

ON CLOUD NiNe

Cloud chemistry (noun). The study of chemical changes that take place in the atmosphere. If your head is in the clouds, this might be the branch of chemistry for you!

I COULDN'T BELIEVE IT was finally Friday and STEM Night.

And I was participating in my first science competition. And Dr. Caroline would be there. My Rube Goldberg machine was working. I had enough lemons. The fan spun perfectly. After testing the machine out a zillion times, I was able to get the tissue paper to turn soggy, which released the plastic arm, which turned on the calculator! My poster board looked better than ever (thank you, Birdie!). Now I just needed to wear something special.

In my bedroom, I pulled on my cable-knit sweater because it was new and blue and looked awesome.

Then I pulled it off.

It was itchy.

I couldn't be scratching myself as I was explaining all about electrons. I had to be a non-itchy person.

I was sure that scientists like Dr. Caroline probably had non-itchy skin.

My dog came up to be scratched. "Hi, Dribble. This is one of the most important nights of my life. And I would love to pet you for ten hours, but I've got to get ready." I put on a cream ribbed turtleneck and skinny jeans. Then I took my turtleneck off again and put on a NASA T-shirt and my lab coat. And of course, I wore the pink cowboy boots my grandparents got me for good luck.

Fifteen minutes later, I hurried downstairs and was raring to go. Mom was already at school. In fact, she had never left. I gazed outside the window. It was five and the sunset was swirls of orange, red, and pink. And in that moment, I wanted to understand everything. Why the sunset was so beautiful. Why my heart was beating so fast. I'm pretty sure it all had to do with chemistry.

"Kate, we don't have to leave for another"—Dad looked at his watch—"thirty minutes."

"I just want to be on time," I said.

"Me too!" shouted Liam. "'Cause I want to make slime."

"All right, you two," said Dad. "Let's go!" Dribble barked.

"I think Dribble wants to go, too!" said Liam.

"He would be a good scientist, don't you think?" said Dad as we piled into the minivan. "He's really curious."

"Yes," I said, "but he might bury and dig up his lab equipment." And we all laughed.

At school, kids and parents milled around the hall. There were tables set up in the corridor and different classrooms were being used as various stations. There was a book fair set up in the library. And a bake sale was in the hallway by the office. It looked like a giant party for science.

I passed by Phoenix and met up with Birdie as we went to the multipurpose room to set up. Banners that said: WHAT DO YOU WANT TO DISCOVER? and SCIENCE ROCKS! were on the far wall. Around the perimeter, tables featured hands-on activities like grow your own crystals, magnets, and a way to make a nimbus cloud out of cotton balls.

"This is going to be so much fun." My eyes scanned the room. "Do you think Dr. Caroline is here yet?"

Birdie shook her head. "I bet she's eating her dinner."

"Imagine. Dr. Caroline eats dinner." I sighed in wonder. "I never thought of her eating like everyone else."

Next I headed into the classroom to get my materials from my cubby. All of my lemons were there but no calculator!

"What!" I shrieked. "How can this be?"

"I'm sorry. This is awful. Maybe you can borrow another calculator," said Biride.

I glanced at the clock on the wall. "It's a particular kind of calculator. One that doesn't use a lot of power. I think this time I've . . . I've got to tell Ms. Daly." I wasn't happy about it, but I didn't see any other way. Without the calculator, there wasn't an end to my project. And I didn't want to embarrass myself in front of Dr. Caroline. That would be even worse than my mom making a big deal about someone trying to mess up my project.

"I think that's a good idea," said Birdie softly.

I raced away, looking for Ms. Daly in the multipurpose room. She was up onstage, talking to—gulp—Dr. Caroline, who was wearing her pink lab coat and had her pink goggles pushed up on top of her head. Her long dark hair was pulled back into a ponytail.

I really wanted to talk with Ms. Daly alone. But there wasn't time. I sped up to her and words rushed out of my mouth. "I can't find your calculator. So my project won't work. Because I need *that* calculator. It uses about 1.5 volts. There's no way my project will work with a fancier calculator! Maybe I should just . . . go home."

Dr. Caroline met my eyes. "Don't give up," she said. "Don't let anyone dim your spark for science." I sort of nodded. I could barely process that I had finally met Dr. Caroline because I was so upset about the missing calculator

Ms. Daly went with me into the classroom. We searched in all of the cubbies. Next we checked the back storage area in the lab. Then she turned to me, a grim look on her face. "I'm afraid it's nowhere to be found."

CHAPTER TWENTY-ONE

MeaSURiNG ReSULtS

Centimeter (noun). A unit of length. It's $1/100$ of a meter and about $2/5$ of an inch. It's part of the metric system, which is based on the power ten. Two, four, six, eight who do we appreciate—ten!

IN THE LAB, I SEARCHED under the tables. Birdie crept into the room and knelt next to me. "Any luck?" she asked.

"Nope. This is all I've found." I opened my hand to reveal an eraser, a bubble gum wrapper, and a piece of lint.

I nodded over at Ms. Daly, who was rummaging

through desk drawers. She looked up. "So far, I've found this." She held a thick black calculator with a large silver screen. "But it's a graphing calculator."

"It will require way too many lemons," I moaned.

"We probably can get your mom to open up the front office," said Ms. Daly. "Maybe there's a calculator in there that might work."

I didn't like the idea of bothering my mom, but . . .

"Tell her," whispered Birdie. "About the person sabotaging you."

"I don't want to be a tattletale," I whispered back.

"At this point, she should know. It's not like you're the one who loses stuff." She half smiled. "That would be me."

I let out a breath. "You're right." I walked over to Ms. Daly and started to explain what really happened. Midway through as I explained the part about *Kate is bad at science*, I realized that Dr. Caroline was standing in the doorway. Dr. Caroline! I closed my mouth.

"Keep going," Dr. Caroline said. "Don't let me stop you. I think it's great to be up-front and honest. And it really makes me sad that someone is completely misunderstanding the point of STEM Night. It's not about winning. It doesn't make you better to put someone down.

And it certainly doesn't make your project better, if you make some else's project worse." Dr. Caroline dug her hands down in her lab coat pockets.

"It's wrong, Kate," said Ms. Daly. "I'm also glad you said something."

"I wish I could do something to help," said Dr. Caroline, her voice full of concern.

That's when I told them about the fingerprints we found using the cocoa powder. Why we were definitely sure that it was someone else. "Because we tested them. Those prints weren't mine."

"I wish we could identify the student from their fingerprints," said Dr. Caroline. "I think it's important that they learn from this."

"I know how to catch the person," said Birdie. "I figured it out because of my ink chromatography experiment. All we would have to do is take the poems off the wall and test the four poems that used blue ink."

"I think we can do that," said Ms. Daly. "I'll just check in with Mrs. Eberlin."

I looked at Birdie. "Thank you," I whispered.

"We haven't caught them yet," she said.

"But we will!"

After Ms. Daly received a text from Mrs. Eberlin with the go-ahead, Birdie took the four poems and with scissors carefully cut out a strip on the very bottom where Mrs. Eberlin had us write the date. The date was about a centimeter from the end of the strip. I like to measure in centimeters because that's how scientists measure stuff—using the metric system.

Birdie hung the strips in the middle of four pencils. "I need four beakers."

"On it," said Ms. Daly, who popped back with four plastic beakers. "Ah," she said. "I think I see where you're going. Continue." She deposited the four beakers on the table.

"Kate, can you fill the beakers with ten milliliters of water?" asked Birdie. "The water is our solvent."

"On it," I said, running to the science lab to grab a graduated cylinder. I sprinted back to the classroom before carefully filling up the beakers. I set them on the table in front of Birdie.

She placed one pencil across each of the four beakers. The bottom of the strip just touched the water. "See, I'm going to let the ink get wet just like I did in my science project."

We watched in amazement as the ink separated. It took about five minutes. "The color patterns are all different," she said. "Let's compare them to the patterns made from the *Kate is bad at science* test strip."

We all stared.

We had a match.

CHAPTER TWENTY-TWO

THE RESPONSIBLE PARTY

Scientific responsibility (noun). The duty of scientists to think about their social responsibilities as well as stick to professional standards. It's like understanding that you can't copy a friend's test but you can help her with her homework.

THE SABOTEUR WAS JEREMY.

It all started to make a little bit of sense. Well, I guess it did. On the soccer field he had doubted my goal. I thought that was just because he was being ultra competitive.

But I realized something. He wanted to beat me on the field *and* at the STEM science fair.

It didn't take Ms. Daly too long to find Jeremy, since he was in front of his poster setting up his empty can of Red Bull.

"Jeremy," said Ms. Daly. "I need to speak with you."

He set down his can. "Okay," he said.

We both followed Ms. Daly into the hallway. After pulling us into the science lab, she calmly explained how we knew that Jeremy was the culprit. Through science, of course.

Jeremy stared at a poster of the periodic table. Then his eyes cut to mine. "Everyone knows you're going to win. It's not fair. Your mom's principal."

Ms. Daly nodded as Jeremy was speaking. "Yes, it's true. Kate's mom *is* the principal. But she has to do her *own* work just like everyone else."

"I work really hard," I blurted out.

"Yeah, and your mom probably makes sure that everyone knows it." Jeremy gestured toward the hall like my mom was standing out there telling teachers I was special.

"Everything you're saying is not true." I shook my head, blinking back some tears.

"I can vouch for that, Jeremy," said Ms. Daly.

111

"I get it. I'm not the principal's kid, so I'm not a VIP." Jeremy sounded hurt.

"I'm sorry you feel overlooked for some reason," said Ms. Daly more gently.

"I don't." He shrugged. But his face looked almost as pale as his hair. "It's not about me. It's about her." His voice warbled.

"Actually, Jeremy," stated Ms. Daly, "this is all about you right now. And your behavior. I think you know that not only is an apology needed, but also, we're going to have to speak to your parents. And there will be consequences. What you did was not acceptable in any way."

Jeremy met my gaze. "I'm sorry, Kate. Really sorry."

"This was all about a silly calculator?" I bit my lip, and then, turning to Ms. Daly, said, "Not that your calculator is silly, Ms. Daly. It's awesome and amazing."

"Well, you went around acting like you were going to win," Jeremy said. "And you don't even know what you're going to do with the prize money."

I felt like he had sucker-punched me. Because it was true. Even though it was STEM Night, I still didn't know what I would do with the money if I won. I was just con-fused. There were so many options and all of them were amazing.

"That doesn't mean I won't figure it out," I said. *If* I won. Now, with all of this drama, I wasn't so sure I would. I felt wobbly.

"I really am sorry," said Jeremy. "I was just mad, I guess."

"Oh," I said. And for a minute, I understood just a little bit. There were things I wanted to do when I was mad, too, that I knew weren't the right thing to do. But I wanted to do them anyway. "No matter what, it wasn't okay to take my stuff. Or write on my poster." My voice grew shaky.

"You're not bad at science," said Jeremy. "You're the opposite."

"Thanks," I breathed.

"Jeremy, I'm afraid your project is disqualified," said Ms. Daly. "STEM Night is a privilege, not a right. I'm going to speak with your parents and you're going to watch but not participate in any activities."

Jeremy's face turned as pink as his strawberry milk. "Okay," he whispered.

For a moment, I felt really sorry for him. He wouldn't be able to enjoy any of the hands-on activities. Outside in the parking lot there was even a telescope for stargazing.

It seemed like Jeremy really did care about his science project a whole lot. He sure had a funny way of showing it, though.

After he handed me the calculator and packed away his poster, I looked away so he wouldn't feel bad. Even though I was still upset at him, I knew what it was like to feel that way. That nothing would work out.

Afterward, I caught up with Birdie in the multipurpose room.

Birdie asked, "How did it go?"

"Fine," I said.

She crossed her fingers. "I hope that nothing else goes wrong."

"Thanks, but right now I don't need luck or superstition. I just need to remember the most important thing—that I love science!"

CHAPTER TWENTY-THREE

TOGETHER WE'RE BETTER

Scientific collaboration (noun). When scientists work together to strengthen their research projects. This means that they share ideas, not that they take their ideas to the gym.

MY VOICE WAS GROWING HOARSE. So many parents, kids, and people had come by to ask me about my Rube Goldberg machine. I answered about a zillion questions.

And I loved it.

It's like the whole world was suddenly science obsessed.

So far three judges had come by—Ms. Daly and our

two fifth grade teachers. They all carried tablets as they scored me and asked a lot of questions.

With a smile, I glanced over at the rows of tables with everyone's posters set up next to one another.

Lights flashed as parents and grandparents took photos.

To my left there was no poster. That was where Jeremy was supposed to be set up.

On the other side of Jeremy's empty spot, Dr. Caroline was talking to Phoenix.

I elbowed Birdie, whose poster was set up to the right of mine. "Look," I whispered. "See who's coming to me next. Okay, I'm calm."

Birdie rolled her eyes. "You're not calm. If you were a crayon, you'd melt."

"Okay, fine. But I'm going to act like it's completely normal. I mean, I know I sort of spoke with her before. But this is different. I'm going to be speaking to Dr. Caroline in person about my project. About *science*!" I smoothed out my lab coat. I hummed. "Just a normal life. Just la dee da."

Birdie nudged me. "Kate. Kate! She's here." I glanced up, right at Dr. Caroline. She had on a really pretty silver chain with a double helix that dangled right in front of me.

"Oh, you're wearing DNA—deoxyribonucleic acid!"

"Yes, I am!"

I glanced down at my lucky pink cowboy boots. "We're both wearing pink!"

"An amazing color," said Dr. Caroline.

"Did you know that anything that has a bluish red to light red color can be considered pink? It can even have slight hints of orange, like in the color salmon, right?" I asked.

"That's right." Dr. Caroline said as she leaned forward. "So, tell me about your project, Kate. How did you choose this idea?"

"I'm fascinated by batteries," I admitted. Even though my voice was steady, my insides weren't. I was a jumble of nerves. But I bravely plowed on. "As a little kid, I was always taking them out of flashlights. The remote control for the TV. Anything. I was just wowed that a tiny little battery could do so much. So, when I discovered that lemons, limes, and apples—oh, and potatoes!—could be used as batteries, I knew I wanted to learn how to do it."

Dr. Caroline smiled and made a note on her iPad.

"But I realized I wanted to do more. So I thought about how I could use batteries in a Rube Goldberg machine. I learned from your show that Rube Goldberg was a fascinating person—a cartoonist, an engineer, and an inventor—who liked to make complicated machines that accomplish simple tasks at the end. And I thought that turning on a calculator is a simple task that scientists do all the time. Plus, you can watch kids and adults make Rube Goldberg machines on YouTube. They're fun and the chain reaction inspires people all over the world to dive into science. And what's better than something that inspires people to become scientists?"

I demonstrated the machine (it worked!) and explained the science of every part of it—the geology behind the pebble, the physics behind dominoes, the size and shape of real strawberries and the properties of beeswax, the water displacement and absorption, and the chemistry of my lemon batteries. After that, I admitted some of the failures along the way. Like forgetting to test my batteries before trying the robot.

"What did you feel like you learned from your mistakes?" asked Dr. Caroline.

"I realized that you learn as much from what doesn't work as you do from what does."

Dr. Caroline nodded. "Cognitive science, which is a special branch that studies the brain, shows that making and discussing mistakes makes us learn faster."

"That's good. My best friend and I also talked a lot about our mess-ups. And helped each other with ideas. The strawberry looks good because of her," I said, pointing to Birdie.

"Well, I'm having trouble not gobbling that strawberry up," said Dr. Caroline. "It looks so real. Your friend is an amazing artist." Dr. Caroline's eyes lit up as she gazed at the chromatography experiment images and drawings on Birdie's poster. "So, you two worked together?"

"Well, we helped each other out," I said.

"Nice. Science is all about collaborations."

Then Dr. Caroline asked me a few more questions before moving on to Birdie. At first, Birdie spoke in a quiet voice, but once she starting talking about getting to see ink separate, her voice grew more and more excited, more confident.

Then she added that chromatography taught her how to catch a crook.

Dr. Caroline took more notes, then she went over to the next aisle to look at Rory's cloud project. I could hear Dr. Caroline's voice. She was pointing and nodding and getting all jazzed about Rory's work too.

I was proud of my project, but, honestly, I was worried about winning. I realized that a lot of other kids did a great job. And that was a good thing. But it meant I had competition with a capital *C*. I thought about what Dr. Caroline had said before, that it wasn't about winning. And I suppose it wasn't, but I still wanted to win anyway.

CHAPTER TWENTY-FOUR

THE WINNING TEAM

Results (noun). The detailed report of your data in a science experiment or inquiry. It might agree with or contradict your hypothesis. That's because in science it's okay to have a wrong hypothesis. Evidence always wins.

"WE ARE SO HAPPY to announce the winners of our fifth grade science competition during our first annual STEM Night," said Ms. Daly. She stood up onstage in the multipurpose room.

In my chair, my legs shook. I'm sure every molecule in my body was shaking, too. Next to me, Birdie bit her lip.

Ms. Daly glanced at the judges who were sitting on

seats up onstage. Dr. Caroline sat in between Mrs. Que and Mrs. Eberlin. Up onstage earlier, Dr. Caroline had already done a whole bunch of demos and they all were awesome. In one of them, she showed how static electricity worked by putting her hands on a silver globe called a Van de Graaff generator. Dr. Caroline's long dark hair was shocked into the air in a way that made it look like she had antenna on her head. In another one, a solution she had created went back and forth between blue and yellow.

It was all awesome, and now the announcement part of the evening was happening. It was exciting, but also nerve-wracking.

"I speak for the entire faculty and staff," continued Ms. Daly, "when I say that we're so proud of our fifth graders. You have stepped up and shown us your hard work. You've asked wonderful questions. Created hypotheses for your experiments and worked hard to create your projects from scratch. You've let nothing get in your way."

That's when Birdie looked at me. And I looked at her. Because that part was true. The only thing that was going to get past us would be subatomic.

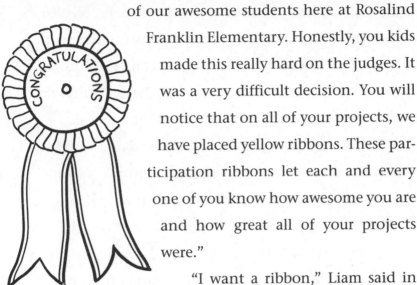

"What impressed the judges is how unique all of the projects were, which reflects the diversity and interests of our awesome students here at Rosalind Franklin Elementary. Honestly, you kids made this really hard on the judges. It was a very difficult decision. You will notice that on all of your projects, we have placed yellow ribbons. These participation ribbons let each and every one of you know how awesome you are and how great all of your projects were."

"I want a ribbon," Liam said in the chair next to me.

"You'll get one," I answered.

"When you're a fifth grader," said Birdie.

He slapped his forehead. "That's in ten hundred years."

"Okay, we're going to hand the mic back over to Dr. Caroline now," said Ms. Daly.

Everyone craned their heads forward.

There were hundreds of people in the room, but it was silent as Dr. Caroline hopped out of her seat.

"Hi, everyone!" said Dr. Caroline, waving.

Liam waved back. "I think she saw me!"

"Okay, it's time to announce our winners," said Dr. Caroline. "I know, like me, you're very eager. But first I want to say that all of you in this room can be scientists." Squinting her eyes, she peered around the packed room.

Liam tapped his chest. "Me?"

"Yes, you," I said, and Liam cheered along with the rest of the crowd.

"All of you can grow up to help make the world a better place," continued Dr. Caroline.

"I want to make it better," Liam admitted.

"Me too," I breathed. Because that was what it was really about. I wanted to use science to help people and our planet.

"And I was impressed with every single project I saw here tonight." Dr. Caroline looked down at her clipboard. "But the winners didn't just have fantastic projects, they also understood the science behind their projects and were able to explain it to me perfectly. So, the third place winner is . . . Avery Cooper!"

Avery jumped out of her chair and raced to the microphone. Dr. Caroline handed her a trophy and an envelope. "Avery's experiment was called Mind Your Beeswax and it was about the science of lip gloss." Dr. Caroline handed the microphone to Avery and she explained a little bit about her project.

"And what will you do for the school community with the prize money?" asked Dr. Caroline.

"I'm going to buy curtains for our theater," said Avery. "My dads can get us a discount."

Everyone applauded.

Okay, only two more opportunities to place. I squeezed my knees together and crossed my fingers. I couldn't look up.

Dr. Caroline smiled so her whole face lit up. "The second place winner is Memito Alvarez for his project Tasty Leather, the science of fruit dehydration."

A cheer went up and I could hear Memito's brothers whistling. Memito jogged up to the podium. Then he bowed as he accepted his trophy and his check. "I'd like to thank the Academy for nominating me for best actor," he joked.

Birdie and I cracked up. Elijah called out, "Best actor in a cooking show!"

"It's funny you should say that," said Memito, pointing at Elijah. "'Cause I'm going to use my prize money to start a cooking club."

Dr. Caroline clapped. "I'm going to have to come back and test out some recipes."

Memito made his way back to his seat with lots of people shaking his hand and slapping his back. Dr. Caroline said, "It's time to announce first place."

My stomach felt hot, like something was starting to boil inside.

"We have a tie for first place," said Dr. Caroline with a huge grin. "Two scientists who embodied the principles of teamwork and support. The winners are Kate Crawford and Brinda 'Birdie' Bhatt. Kate's project, a Rube Goldberg machine called Lemon Power, included multiple scientific principles and, after many moving parts, ended with a calculator being turned on. Birdie's project was Color Sleuthing, which looked at the wonder of ink chromatography." The audience cheered and thundered their applause.

Birdie and I locked eyes before launching ourselves

out of our seats for a big hug. I was glad for all that chemistry taking place to power our muscles.

"They won not just for their projects," continued Dr. Caroline, "which were awesome, by the way, but because the two of them used what they knew about science and applied it to everyday life, and they helped each other make their projects better."

As we walked up to the front, I knew there was a tiny part of me that didn't like sharing first place. But if I had to share it with anyone, it would be with my best friend Birdie.

After we both got to share a little bit more about our projects, Dr. Caroline asked what we would do with our money.

"I would like to make a mural on the brick wall facing the playground," said Birdie. "And I'll need lots of helpers."

I could hear Liam's voice cheering—mine too.

"And Kate, what about you?" I was about to say *I'm going to upgrade the science lab*, but then I got an idea.

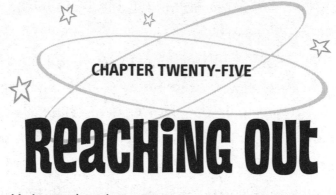

CHAPTER TWENTY-FIVE

ReaCHiNG OUt

Liquid nitrogen (noun). The liquid form of nitrogen. It's super cold. So cold that it could burn you. Just like you would never drink boiling oil, you'd never drink this. It's *that* cold.

"I WANT TO USE MY MONEY to do a livestreaming event," I said. "Maybe we could do science experiments on the internet like you do, Dr. Caroline. I could use my prize money to get all of the materials we'd need, and people might like them so much that they'd donate to the school. And maybe we could raise enough money to fund everyone's ideas. Phoenix could get composting bins for the garden and Elijah could start a battle of the bands!"

"Woo-boy!" Dr. Caroline put her hand up to her forehead like it was blazing hot. "That's a lot of ideas."

"We have two fifth grade classes," said Birdie. "So forty of them."

"You want to do a science show like mine?" asked Dr. Caroline, after she was quiet for a moment. I nodded. She looked like she was thinking about something and then smiled. "Let's do it! Let's do it here and now. And it won't cost a thing. You can use your prize money as the first donation for the event. Let me just set up the livestreaming funding app on my phone, and we'll see what science fans all over the world will donate to fund these awesome ideas—ideas that will give you all even more learning opportunities. Plus, I've got the perfect bonus demo."

She grabbed her phone. "While I'm doing this, why don't the rest of you take a five-minute water break?"

That's when Jeremy came up to me. He hung his head. "I'm so, so sorry, Kate. For messing everything up. I think you really did figure out the best way to use the prize money."

"Thanks," I said. "I hope this works and we can get those soccer goals you want."

Jeremy nodded and I could see his parents standing nearby looking pretty serious. I'm sure he was going to get a very big lecture when he got home tonight.

Dr. Caroline went back to the microphone. "Okay, everyone, it's time for our demo. And for our livestream fundraiser to begin."

Dr. Caroline made a few taps on her cell phone and before we knew it, we were livestreaming a fundraiser in our multipurpose room. She asked our AV guru, Ms. Gottfried, to film.

Dr. Caroline looked at both Birdie and me. "I want you two to stand up onstage. We're going to make a cloud."

That seemed just perfect. Because I was already on cloud nine. That means your happy place, according to my dad. Only Dr. Caroline was going to make an actual cloud.

"This is my all-time favorite demo," said Dr. Caroline. "And it's my finale. Because I've gotta catch a plane home tonight!"

The idea of Dr. Caroline leaving made me a little sad. But only just a smidge. Because there I was standing next to Dr. Caroline, who was about to do her favorite demo ever. With me. I just knew I would remember this day for the rest of my life.

"We're going to make actual clouds inside the multi-purpose room?" asked Birdie, who looked just as wowed as the audience.

"Yes! Yes!" I was already clapping.

"So right there you have a bucket of liquid nitrogen," said Dr. Caroline. She pointed to the white bucket.

I knew that was when nitrogen, usually a gas, was cooled so much that it became a liquid. "It's super cold!" I said.

"Exactly!" exclaimed Dr. Caroline. "Almost negative 200 degrees Celsius. Don't touch it or drink it. Safety first. That's why I'm handing you all goggles"—I took a pink pair and Birdie grabbed a blue one—"and cryogenic gloves to protect your hands. And in this blue bucket I have hot water at about 80 degrees Celsius."

"Hot!" I said, blowing up my cheeks. That's about 175° F. So, really hot!

"Are you ready for this?" asked Dr. Caroline.

"Oh yes!" I shouted.

"So ready!" said Birdie.

Dr. Caroline asked us to stand a few steps behind

her as she put her goggles firmly on her head. "So you girls are going to count to three backward for me."

"Three. Two. One!" we cried.

And then Dr. Caroline poured the hot water into the bucket of nitrogen.

There was a loud crackly sound.

A cloud poofed into the air. It was so thick that I couldn't even see my gloves.

"Oh, look look!" I shouted. "The liquid nitrogen turned into a gas. So cool!"

Ms. Gottfried tossed Dr. Caroline her phone so that she could start filming from behind the cloud. The crowd gasped and hooted and hollered.

"That was beautiful," sighed Birdie. Kids and parents were out of their seats. The applause was super loud.

"Nice job on the countdown, girls!" said Dr. Caroline. "What kind of change was that?"

"A phase change!" I shouted.

"That's right!" said Dr. Caroline. "The nitrogen molecules stayed the same, but the phase changed from liquid to gas."

"Gas takes up more space than

the liquid," I said, looking up as the clouds of vapor started to disappear.

"Exactly," said Dr. Caroline. "The molecules are more separated. And when they move from gas to liquid, the molecules go from far apart to close together."

"Just like when farm dogs herd sheep," added Birdie.

"That's right! You guys are a great team," said Dr. Caroline. She glanced at her phone. "Guess what?! We definitely raised enough money to fund every kid's idea. And maybe a little to help out with the STEM Night next year." She pumped her arm into the air.

Everyone cheered. Some people stomped on the floor with their feet.

"Science is awesome," I said.

"You can say that again," said Dr. Caroline.

"Science is awesome!" we all cheered.

Dr. Caroline shut down the fundraising app and put her phone in her lab coat pocket. "Thanks so much for having me here tonight, folks. Now go out and have more fun. There are tons of hands-on stations. Stay curious!"

Since science was involved—that definitely wouldn't be a problem.

LEMON-LIME CLOCK

MATERIALS:

☆ 3 lemons
☆ 3 limes
☆ 6 galvanized nails
☆ 6 pieces of copper wire (or 6 pre-1982 pennies)
☆ 7 alligator clips
☆ 1 digital clock
☆ Pliers (if using wire instead of pennies)

PROTOCOL:

1. If you're using wire instead of pennies, use the pliers to cut 6 pieces of wire, each about 2 inches long.

2. Plunge 1 nail into the left side of the first lime [NAIL 1].

3. Plunge 1 copper wire (or penny) into the right side of the first lime [COPPER 1].

4. Plunge 1 nail into the left side of the first lemon [NAIL 2].

5. Plunge 1 copper wire (or penny) into the right side of the first lemon [COPPER 2].

6. Plunge 1 nail into the left side of the second lime [NAIL 3].

7. Plunge 1 copper wire (or penny) into the right side of the second lime [COPPER 3].

8. Plunge 1 nail into the left side of the second lemon [NAIL 4].

9. Plunge 1 copper wire (or penny) into the right side of the second lemon [COPPER 4].

10. Plunge 1 nail into the left side of the third lime [NAIL 5].

11. Plunge 1 copper wire (or penny) into the right side of the third lime [COPPER 5].

12. Plunge 1 nail into the left side of the third lemon [NAIL 6].

13. Plunge 1 copper wire (or penny) into the right side of the third lemon [COPPER 6].

14. Use one alligator clip to connect NAIL 1 and COPPER 2.

15. Use one alligator clip to connect NAIL 2 and COPPER 3.

16. Use one alligator clip to connect NAIL 3 and COPPER 4.

17. Use one alligator clip to connect NAIL 4 and COPPER 5.

18. Use one alligator clip to connect NAIL 5 and COPPER 6.

19. Remove the battery cover and the battery to expose the positive/negative side of the clock.

20. Use another alligator clip to connect NAIL 6 to the negative side of the clock.

21. Use the last alligator clip to connect COPPER 1 to the positive side of the clock.

22. Enjoy your Lemon-Lime Clock!

HOW IT WORKS:

Our lemons and limes form a battery that is strong enough to power a small digital clock. For it to work properly, the negative terminal on the clock must be connected to the nail, and the positive terminal must be connected to the copper wire. The electrons travel from the zinc through the lemon/

lime to the copper electrode. From here, they move through the wire to the neighboring zinc electrode to repeat this process. The electrons eventually leave the last lemon/lime through the wire to the digital clock. What happens when you reverse the alligator clips? This action stops the natural flow of electrons from high energy to low energy. Batteries work as a result of the spontaneous travel of electrons from metal to metal; the electrons cannot flow in the opposite direction unless they have an external power source (like a battery). Can you imagine plugging your lemons and limes into the wall to recharge them?

DR. Kate Biberdorf, also known as Kate the Chemist by her fans, is a science professor at UT–Austin by day and a science superhero by night (well, she does that by day, too). Kate travels the country building a STEM army of kids who love science as much as she does. You can often find her breathing fire or making slime—always in her lab coat and goggles.

You can visit Kate on Instagram and Facebook @KatetheChemist, on Twitter @K8theChemist, and online at KatetheChemist.com.